FRANKIE PICKLE™
AND THE CLOSET OF DOOM

written and illustrated by
ERIC WIGHT

SIMON & SCHUSTER
BOOKS FOR YOUNG READERS
New York   London   Toronto   Sydney

SIMON & SCHUSTER BOOKS FOR YOUNG READERS
An imprint of Simon & Schuster Children's Publishing Division
1230 Avenue of the Americas, New York, New York 10020
This book is a work of fiction. Any references to historical events, real people, or real locales are used fictitiously. Other names, characters, places, and incidents are products of the author's imagination, and any resemblance to actual events or locales or persons, living or dead, is entirely coincidental.

For information about special discounts for bulk purchases, please contact Simon & Schuster Special Sales at 1-866-506-1949 or business@simonandschuster.com.
The Simon & Schuster Speakers Bureau can bring authors to your live event. For more information or to book an event, contact the Simon & Schuster Speakers Bureau at 1-866-248-3049 or visit our website at www.simonspeakers.com.
Also available in a Simon & Schuster Books for Young Readers hardcover edition
Book design by Eric Wight and Lizzy Bromley
The text for this book is set in Farao.
The illustrations for this book are rendered digitally.
Manufactured in the United States of America
0313 MTN
First Simon & Schuster Books for Young Readers paperback edition May 2010
8 10 9 7
The Library of Congress has cataloged the hardcover edition as follows:
Wight, Eric, 1974–
Frankie Pickle and the closet of doom / written and illustrated by Eric Wight.
p. cm.—(Frankie Pickle)
Summary: Fourth-grader Frankie Piccolini has a vivid imagination when it comes to cleaning his disastrously messy room, but eventually even he decides that it is just too dirty.
ISBN 978-1-4169-6484-1 (paper over board : alk. paper)
[1. Cleanliness—Fiction. 2. Orderliness—Fiction. 3. Imagination—Fiction. 4. Family life—Fiction. 5. Dogs—Fiction.] I. Title.
PZ7.W6392C1 2009
[Fic]—dc22
2008030865
ISBN 978-1-4424-1304-7 (pbk)
ISBN 978-1-4424-1307-8 (eBook)

To Ethan & Abbie,
my greatest adventure

FRANKIE PICKLE™

AND THE CLOSET OF DOOM

CHAPTER ONE

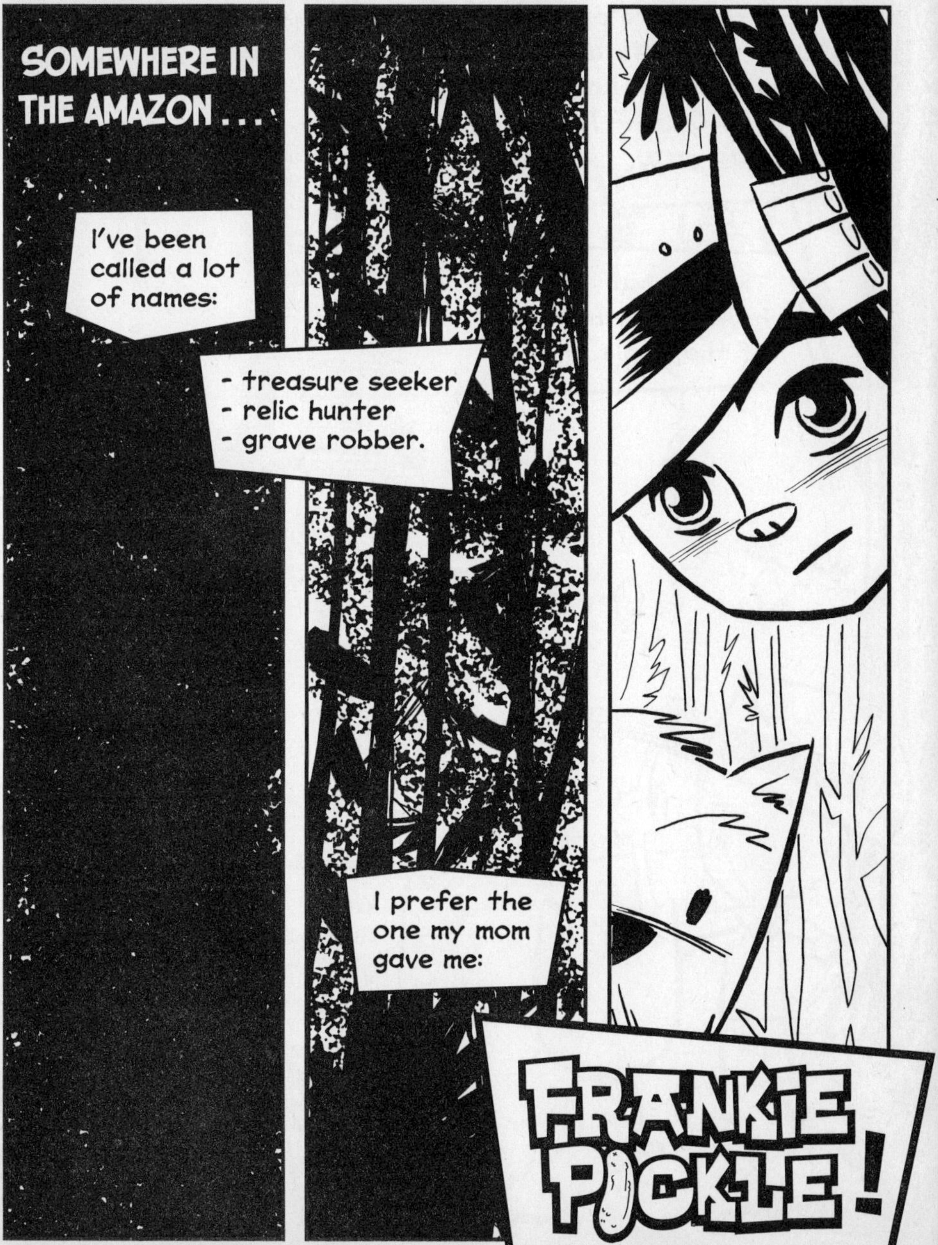
SOMEWHERE IN THE AMAZON . . .
I've been called a lot of names:
- treasure seeker
- relic hunter
- grave robber.
I prefer the one my mom gave me:
FRANKIE PICKLE!

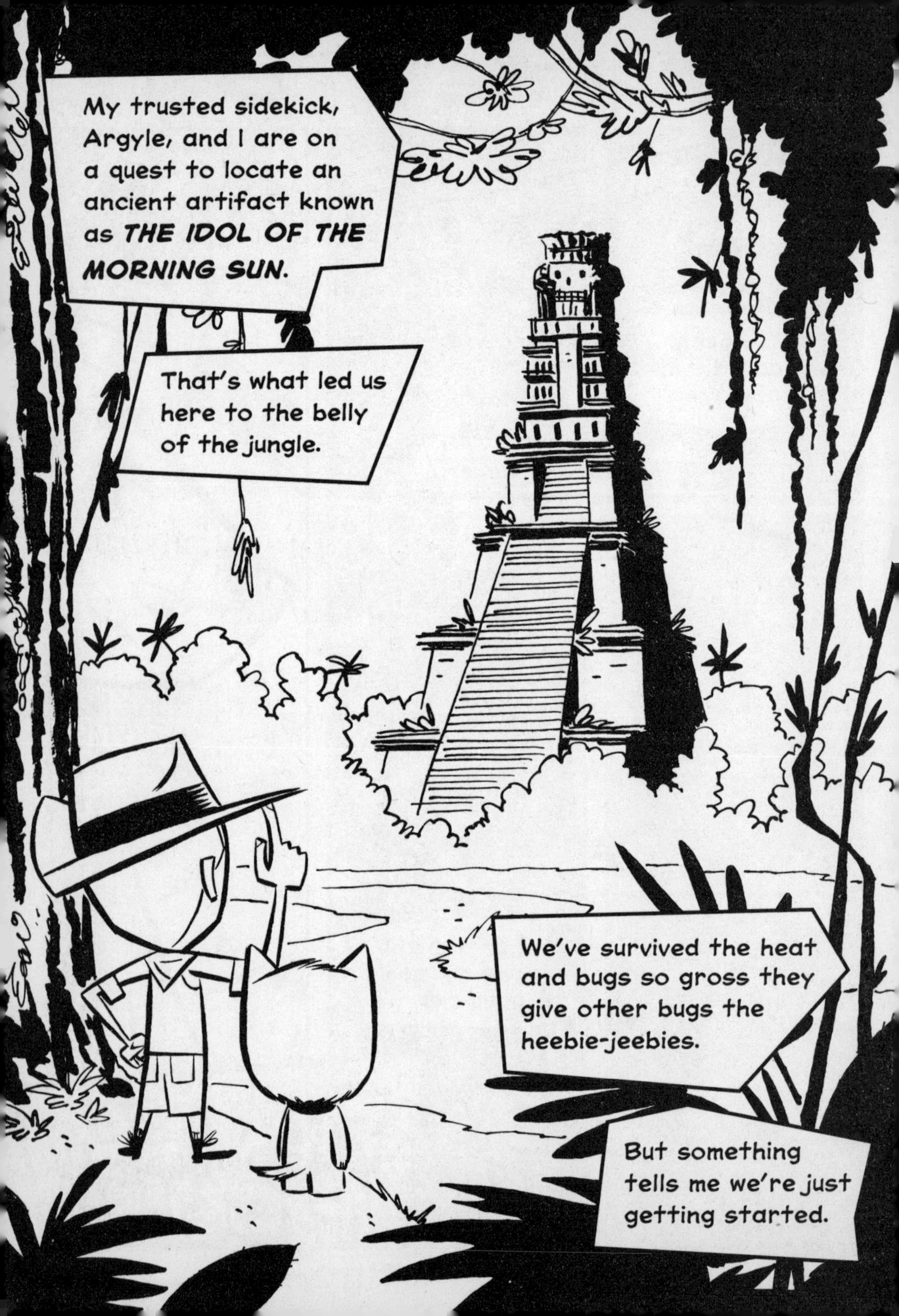
My trusted sidekick, Argyle, and I are on a quest to locate an ancient artifact known as ***THE IDOL OF THE MORNING SUN.***
That's what led us here to the belly of the jungle.
We've survived the heat and bugs so gross they give other bugs the heebie-jeebies.
But something tells me we're just getting started.

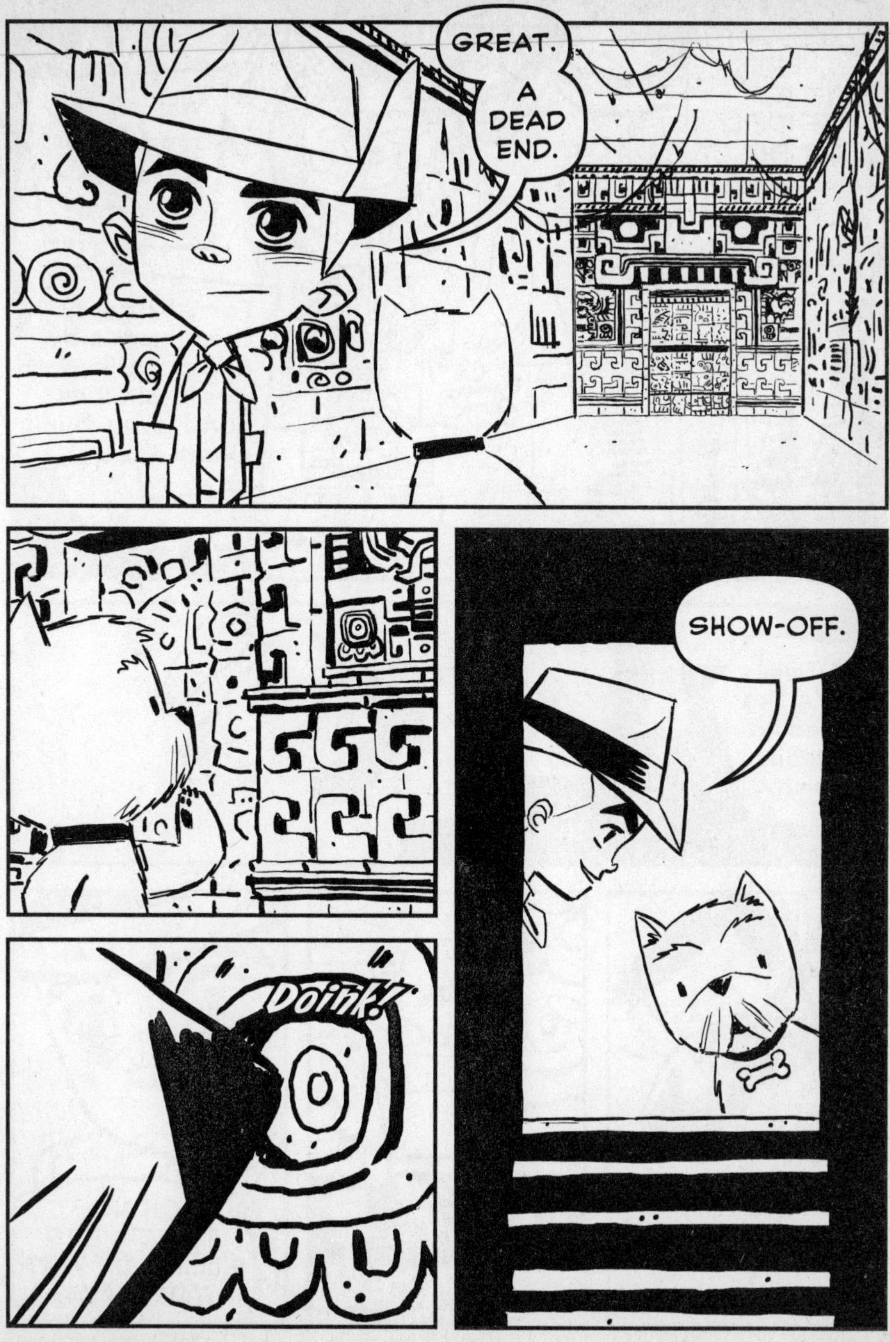
GREAT.
A DEAD END.
Doink!
SHOW-OFF.

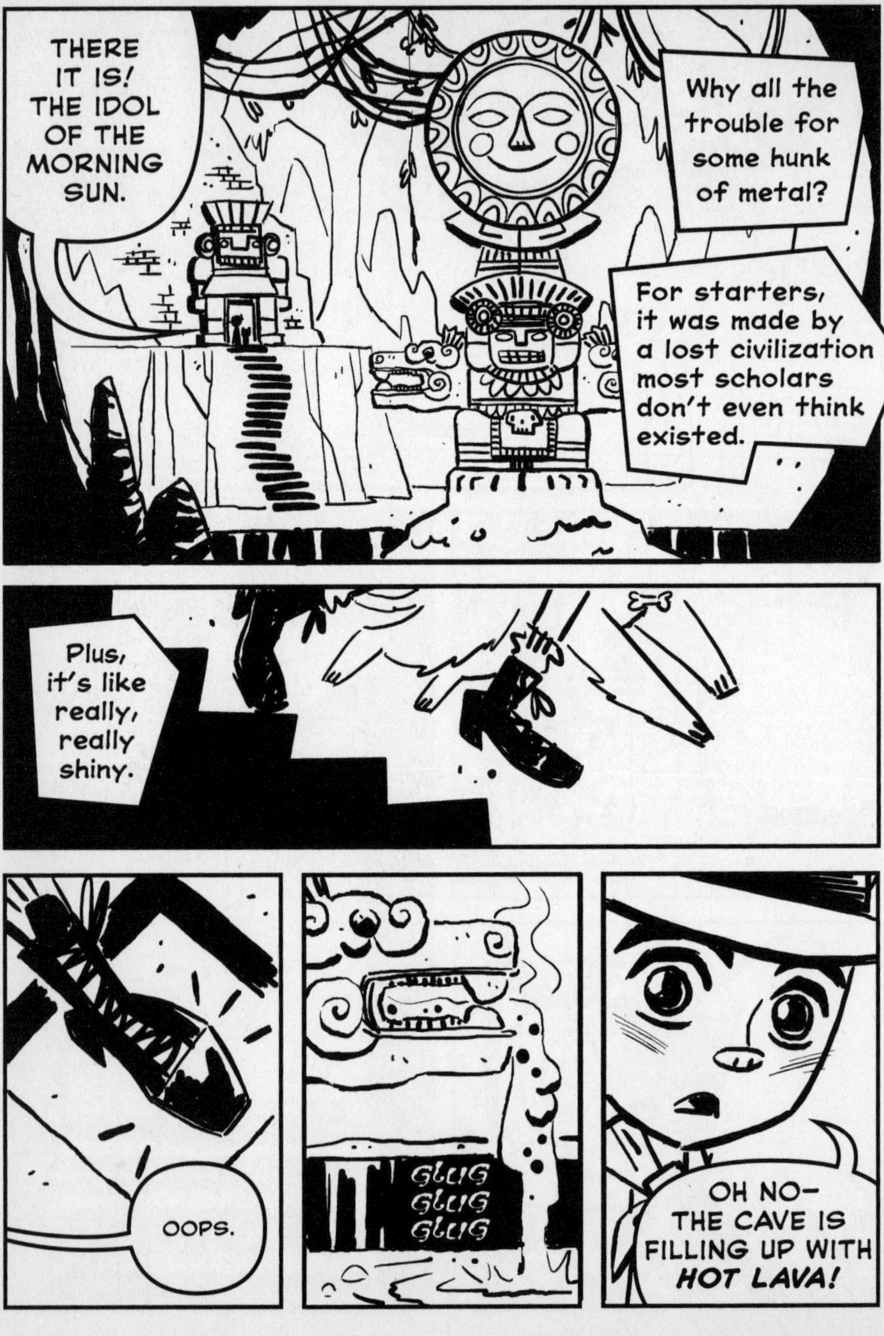
THERE IT IS! THE IDOL OF THE MORNING SUN.
Why all the trouble for some hunk of metal?
For starters, it was made by a lost civilization most scholars don't even think existed.
Plus, it's like really, really shiny.
OOPS.
GLUG GLUG GLUG
OH NO— THE CAVE IS FILLING UP WITH *HOT LAVA!*

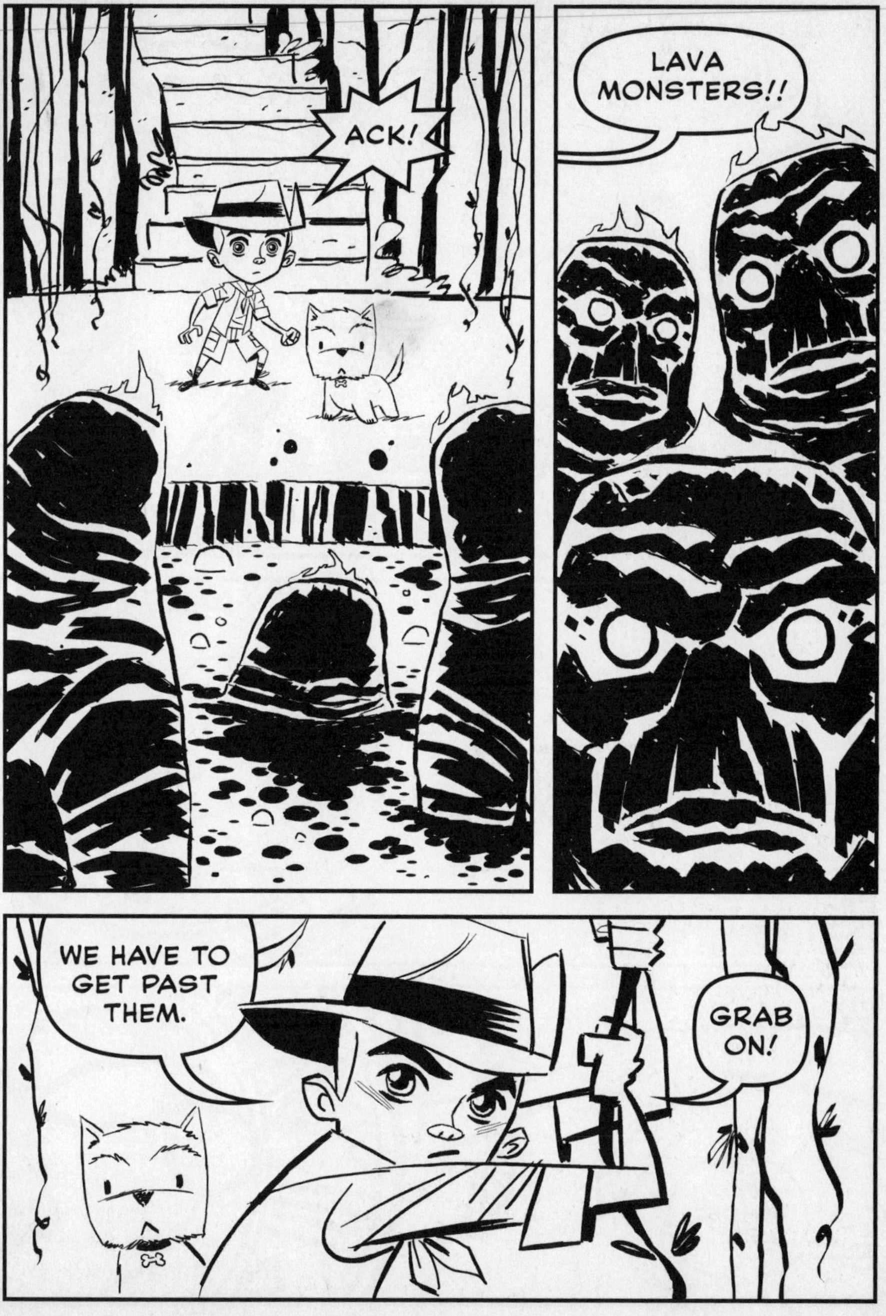
ACK!
LAVA MONSTERS!!
WE HAVE TO GET PAST THEM.
GRAB ON!

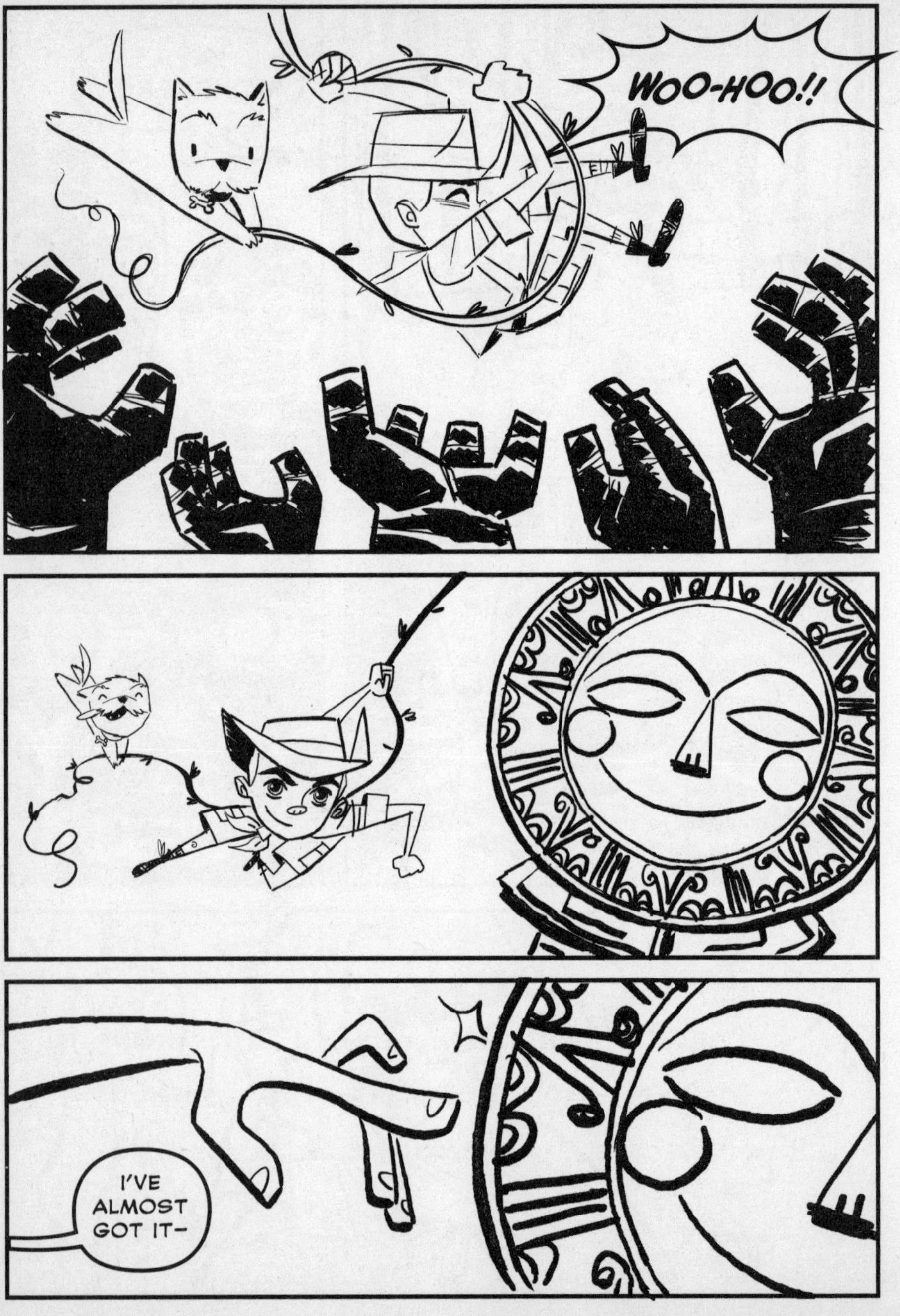
WOO-HOO!!
I'VE ALMOST GOT IT–

CHAPTER TWO

Frankie reached across the breakfast table to claim his prize: a goldenly delicious waffle. The only problem was, someone else got it first.

"Leggo, Bro," said Frankie's older sister Piper as she snatched the last waffle. Piper was the sporty one in the family:

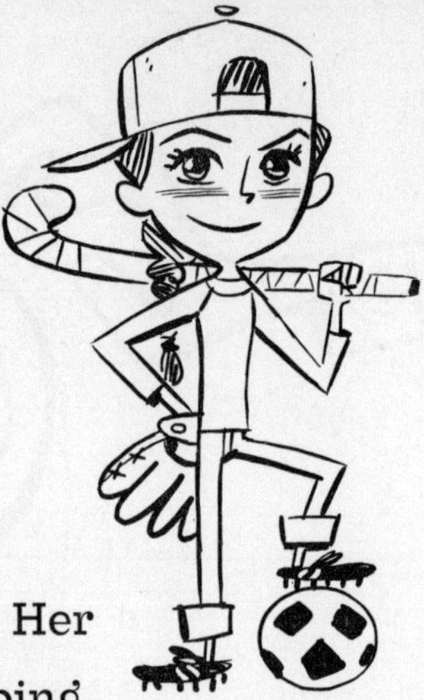

softball, soccer, tennis, field hockey—pretty much anything that involved hitting or kicking.

"Lurgle burgle," said Frankie's younger sister Lucy. Lucy was the diaper-wearing one in the family. Her skills included eating, sleeping, burping, and being cute. She was an expert at all of them.

"You keep out of this," Frankie said to Lucy. "You can't even chew solid food yet."

"Morning, Champ," Dad said, ruffling Frankie's hair. "I'm about to whip up another batch."

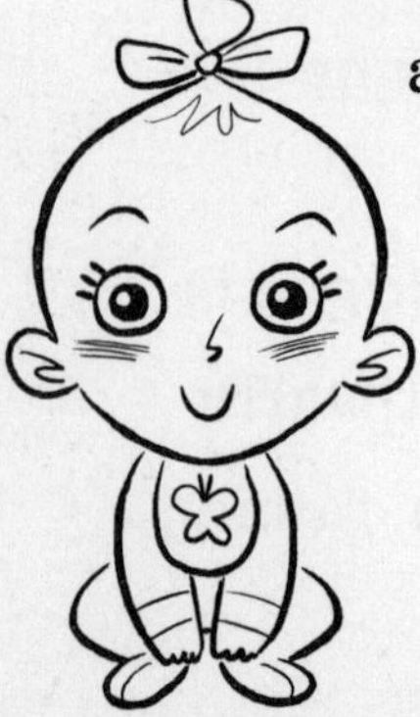

"No time," Frankie said. He dug through the pantry. Score! A Toaster Tart. "I'll eat this on the way to Kenny's house."

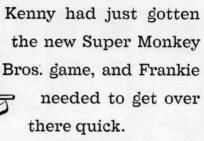

Kenny had just gotten the new Super Monkey Bros. game, and Frankie needed to get over there quick.

Blocking his path to the front door was a laundry basket with legs.

"Not so fast, Franklin Lorenzo Piccolini," said the basket.

Not the Middle Name! Frankie froze in his tracks.

Mom set down the basket. "You're not going anywhere until you CLEAN UP YOUR ROOM," she said.

Frankie gulped. Lava monsters didn't seem so scary compared to Mom.

CHAPTER THREE

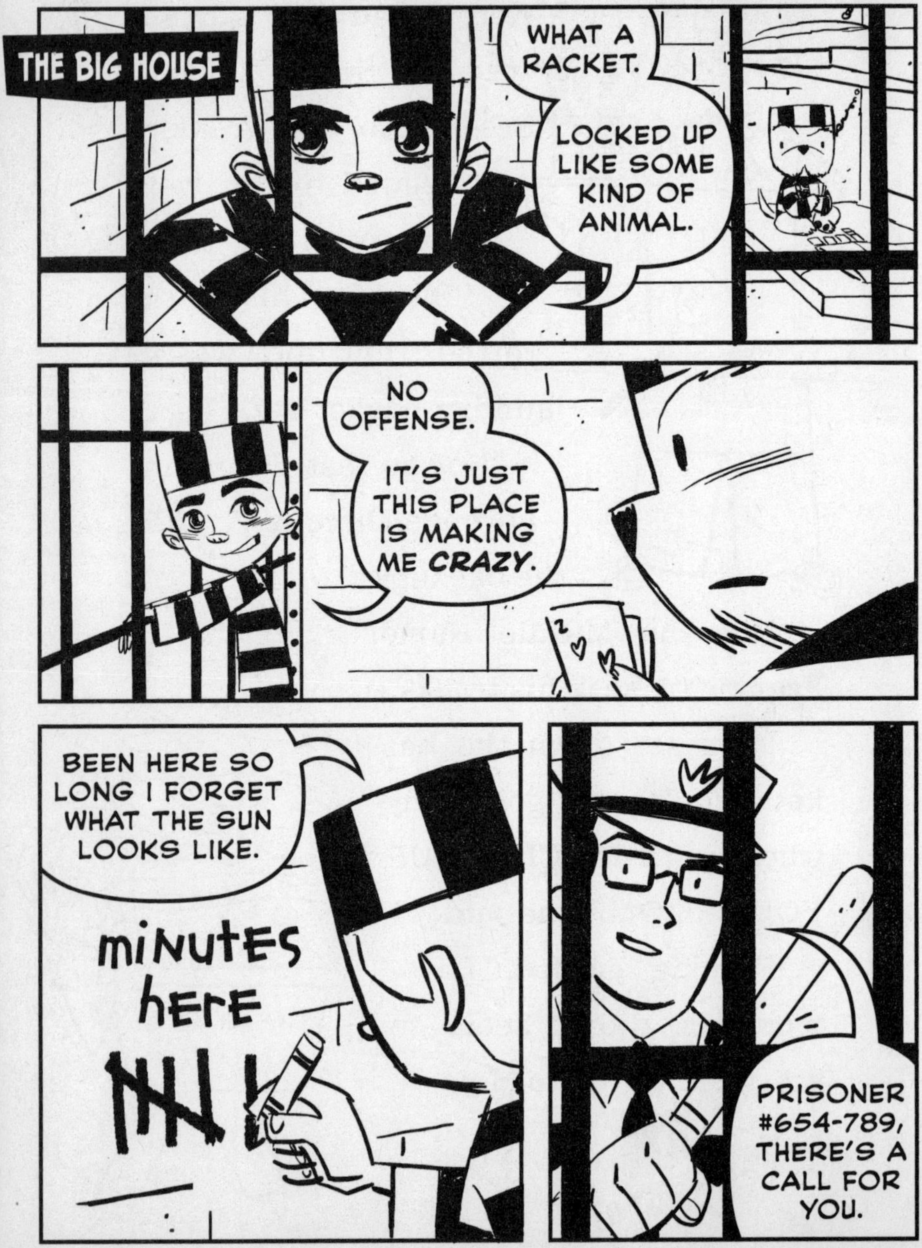
THE BIG HOUSE
WHAT A RACKET.
LOCKED UP LIKE SOME KIND OF ANIMAL.
NO OFFENSE.
IT'S JUST THIS PLACE IS MAKING ME *CRAZY*.
BEEN HERE SO LONG I FORGET WHAT THE SUN LOOKS LIKE.
minutes here
PRISONER #654-789, THERE'S A CALL FOR YOU.

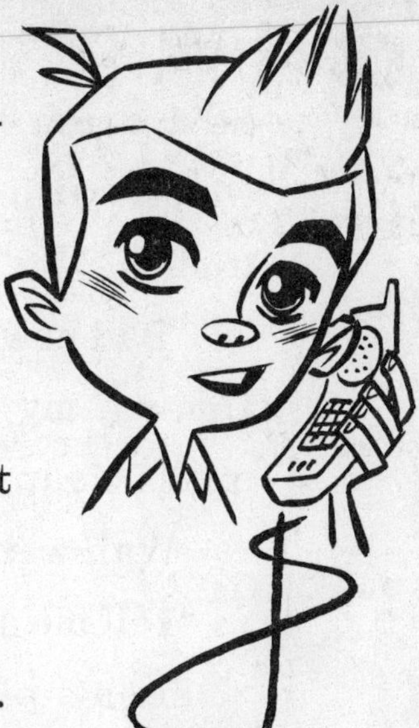

"And that better be washable crayon on the wall," Dad said as he handed Frankie the telephone.

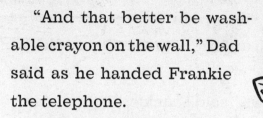

"Hello?" said Frankie.

"Da-da-da!" said a trumpet on the other end of the line.

"Hey, Kenny."

Kenny didn't talk much.

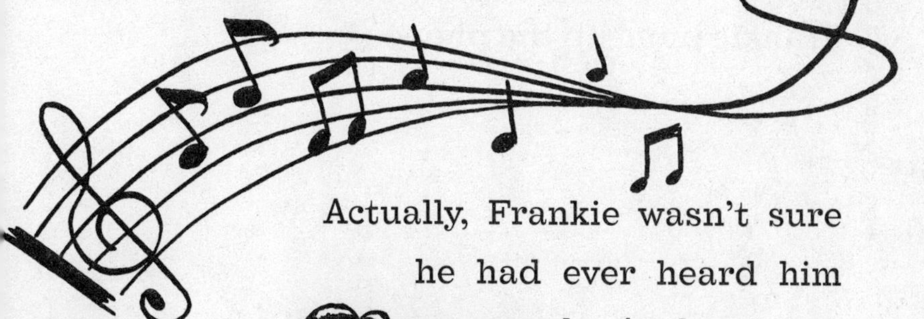

Actually, Frankie wasn't sure he had ever heard him speak. At least not with words. Kenny said it all with music. If he didn't have an instrument,

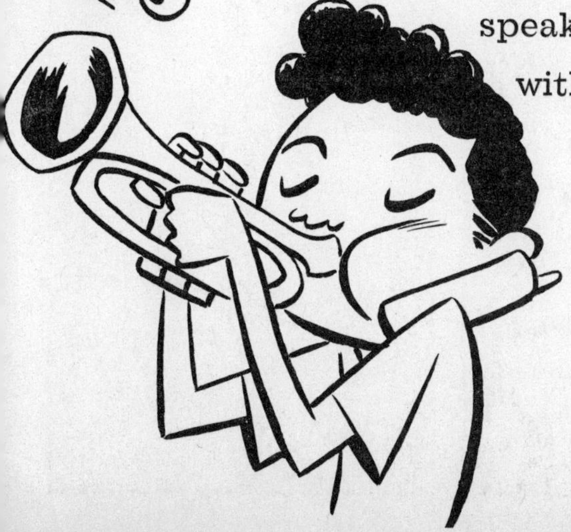

he'd drum his pencil or tap his foot or whistle with a blade of grass. Kenny played it all.

"Bad news," said Frankie. "The warden—I mean, my mom—says I can't come over until I clean my room."

"Wah-wah wah-waaaaaah," said Kenny.

"Tell me about it. I'll catch you later."

Kenny played a tune for good luck. Frankie hung up the phone.

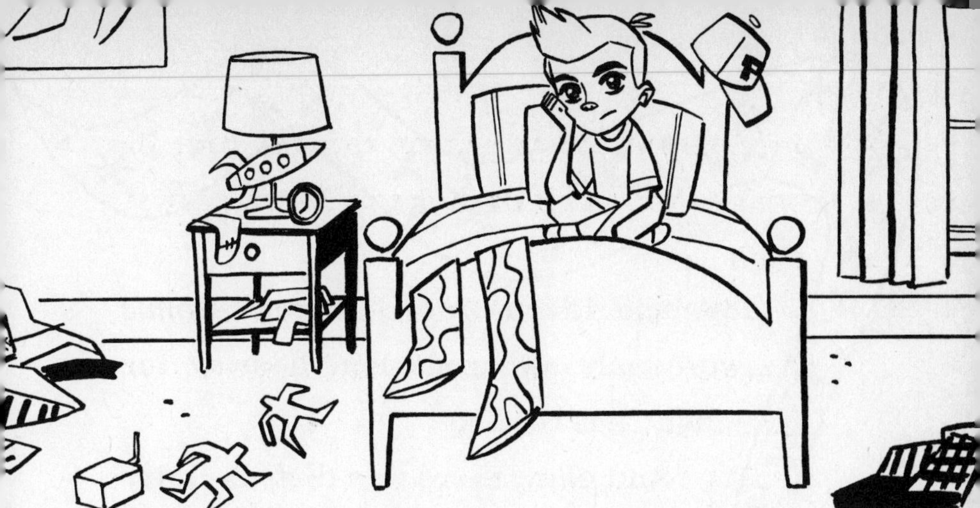

CHAPTER FOUR

Frankie sat on his bed, staring at his room.

A "disaster," Mom called it.

That was just how Frankie liked it.

Sure, his action figures were scattered everywhere. That made it easy to continue from whatever cliffhanger he left them in. Yes, his comics were piled in a big heap next to his bed. But that meant the

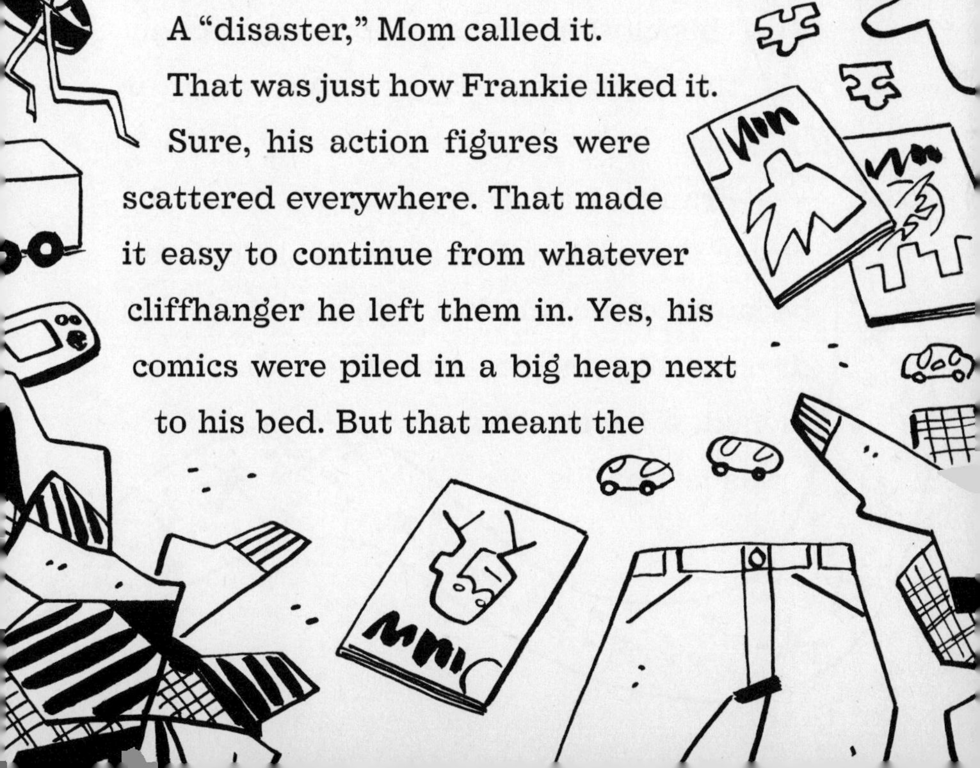

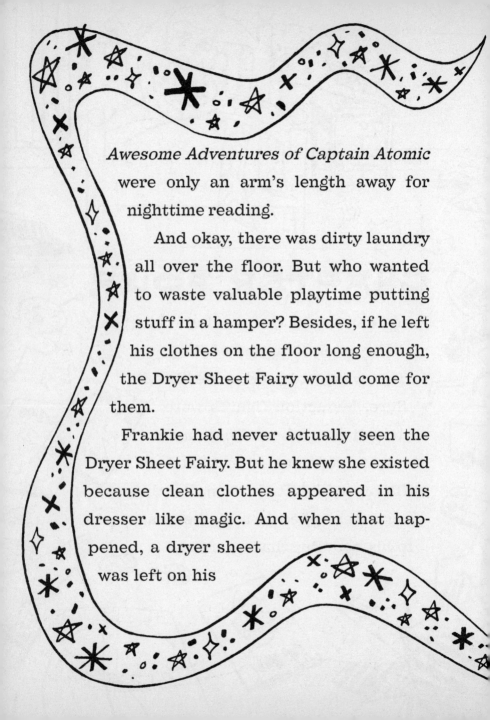

Awesome Adventures of Captain Atomic were only an arm's length away for nighttime reading.

And okay, there was dirty laundry all over the floor. But who wanted to waste valuable playtime putting stuff in a hamper? Besides, if he left his clothes on the floor long enough, the Dryer Sheet Fairy would come for them.

Frankie had never actually seen the Dryer Sheet Fairy. But he knew she existed because clean clothes appeared in his dresser like magic. And when that happened, a dryer sheet was left on his

pillow like a sprinkle of pixie dust. Frankie was collecting them to make an April Fresh superhero cape.

If only he had magical powers like the Dryer Sheet Fairy. Cleaning his room would be a breeze. He bet she could pick up dirty clothes using only her mind.

Wait. What if he could do that too? Frankie had been wishing for superpowers every birthday since he was five. It was worth a try.

He focused on a heap of clothes.

Nothing.

Maybe he wasn't trying enough. He concentrated harder.

Still nothing.

But then . . .

A pair of sweatpants began to wiggle.

It was working!

CHAPTER FIVE

All those birthday wishes had finally paid off. Frankie had been hoping to be able to fly or stop time, but moving laundry with your mind was cool too.

Go into the hamper, he repeated in his head. The sweatpants wiggled some more. He stared so hard, his eyes were drying out. The pile started to rise. Up . . . and up . . . and . . .

A shaggy white dog shook off the clothes he had been sleeping under. Argyle stretched, letting out a roar of a yawn.

"Figures it was you," said Frankie.

He supposed it was time to clean his room like a nonsuperhero.

Frankie shoved everything he could into his closet, until it was so full he was afraid the hinges might pop off. Clothes, books, toys—it didn't matter. As long as Mom could no longer see it, it was clean enough for him.

He stepped back to admire his progress. Barely a dent. This was going to take FOREVER.

Grabbing his sweatpants from under Argyle, Frankie rolled them into a ball and tossed it at the hamper. Instead of sinking a three-pointer, he sunk the whole basket. Clothes spilled onto the floor. Something else did too. Something shiny, with arms and legs and a turbo-rocket jet pack.

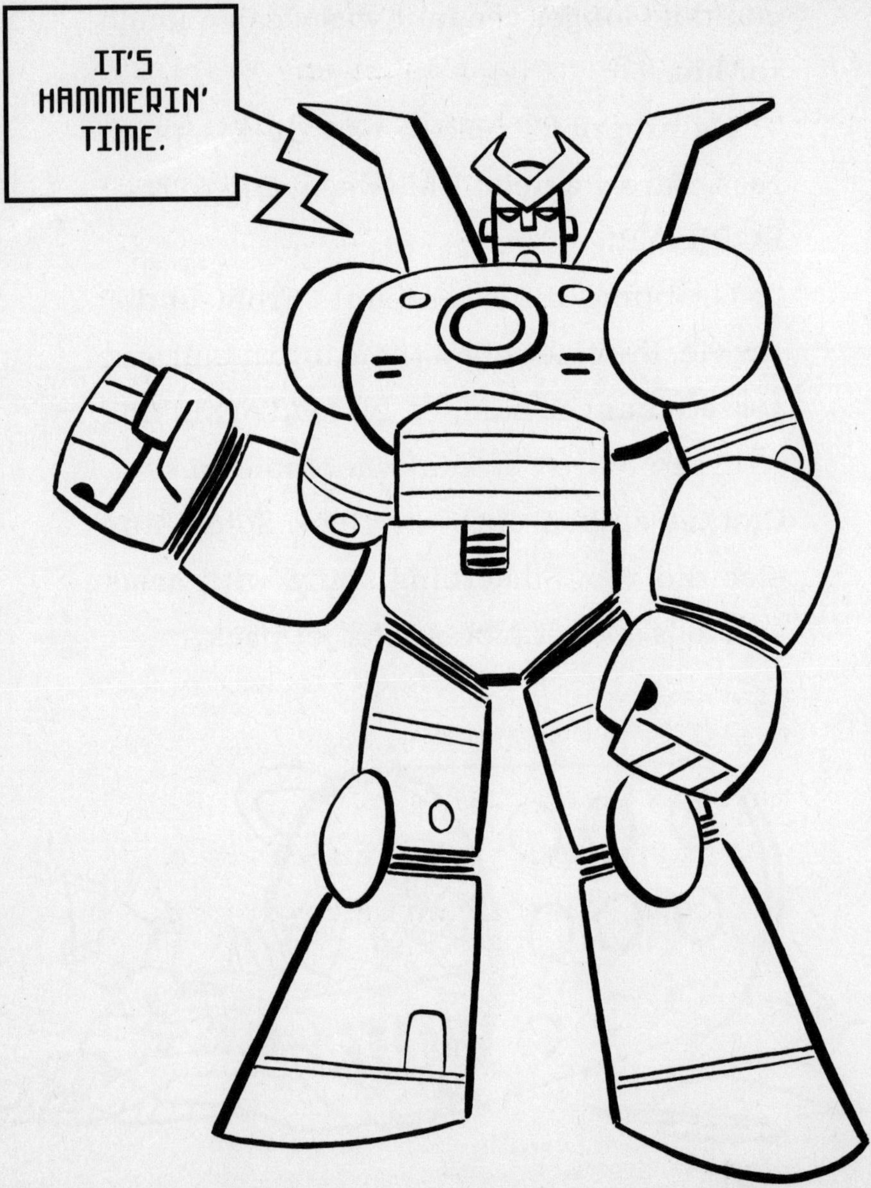
IT'S HAMMERIN' TIME.

"GoGo Robo!" Frankie shouted.

GoGo Robo wasn't just any robot. He was the robot with the Battle-Action Kung-Fu Kick.™ And if you pushed the button on his jet pack, he said cool things like, "Prepare to be scrapped," and "It's hammerin' time."

GoGo Robo must have gotten tossed into the hamper by mistake. A perfect example of why cleaning rooms was a bad idea.

Frankie stomped around like his favorite robot, looking for a challenger to do battle with. Hanging on the back of his door was the dryer sheet cape.

A smile curled across Frankie's face.

Cleaning his room would have to wait.

CHAPTER SIX

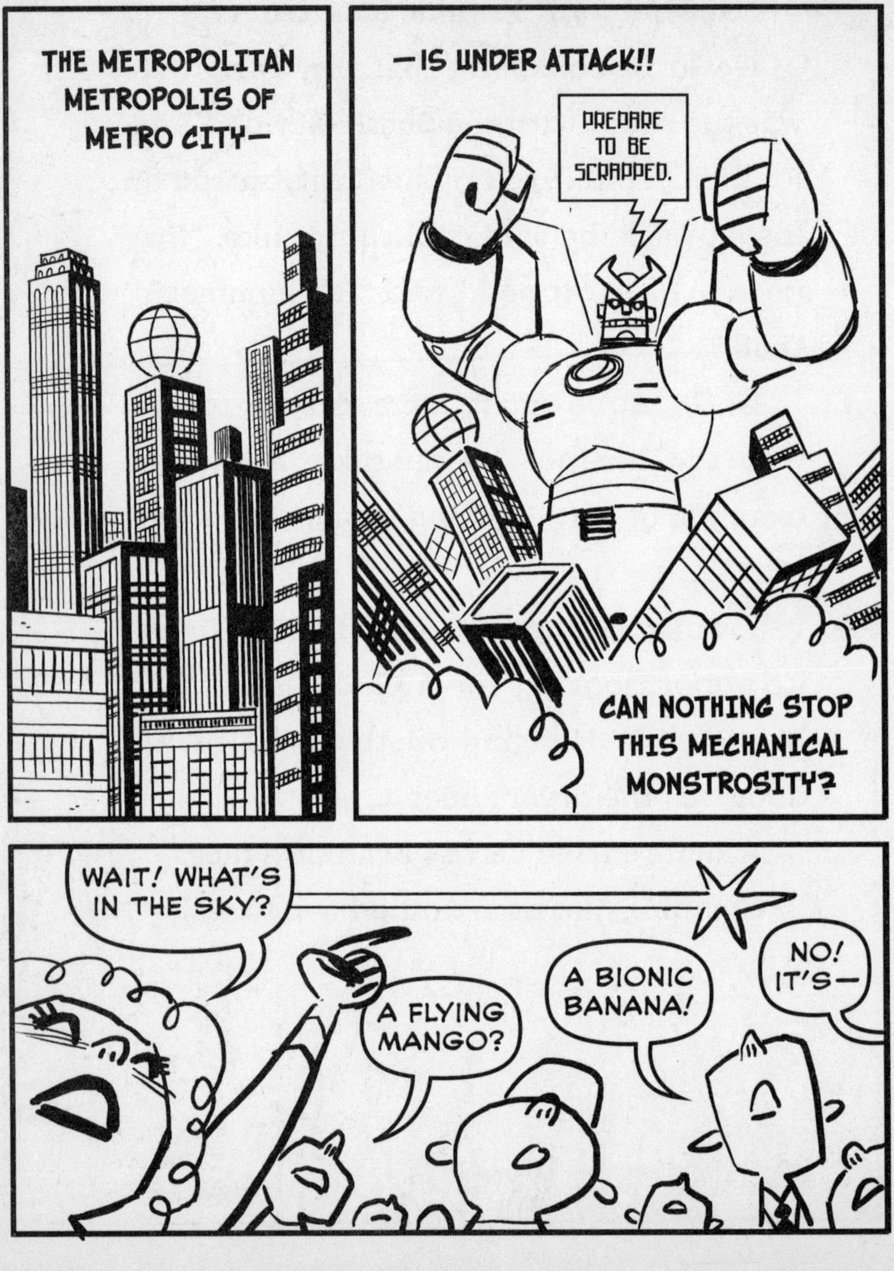
THE METROPOLITAN METROPOLIS OF METRO CITY—
—IS UNDER ATTACK!!
PREPARE TO BE SCRAPPED.
CAN NOTHING STOP THIS MECHANICAL MONSTROSITY?
WAIT! WHAT'S IN THE SKY?
A FLYING MANGO?
A BIONIC BANANA!
NO! IT'S—

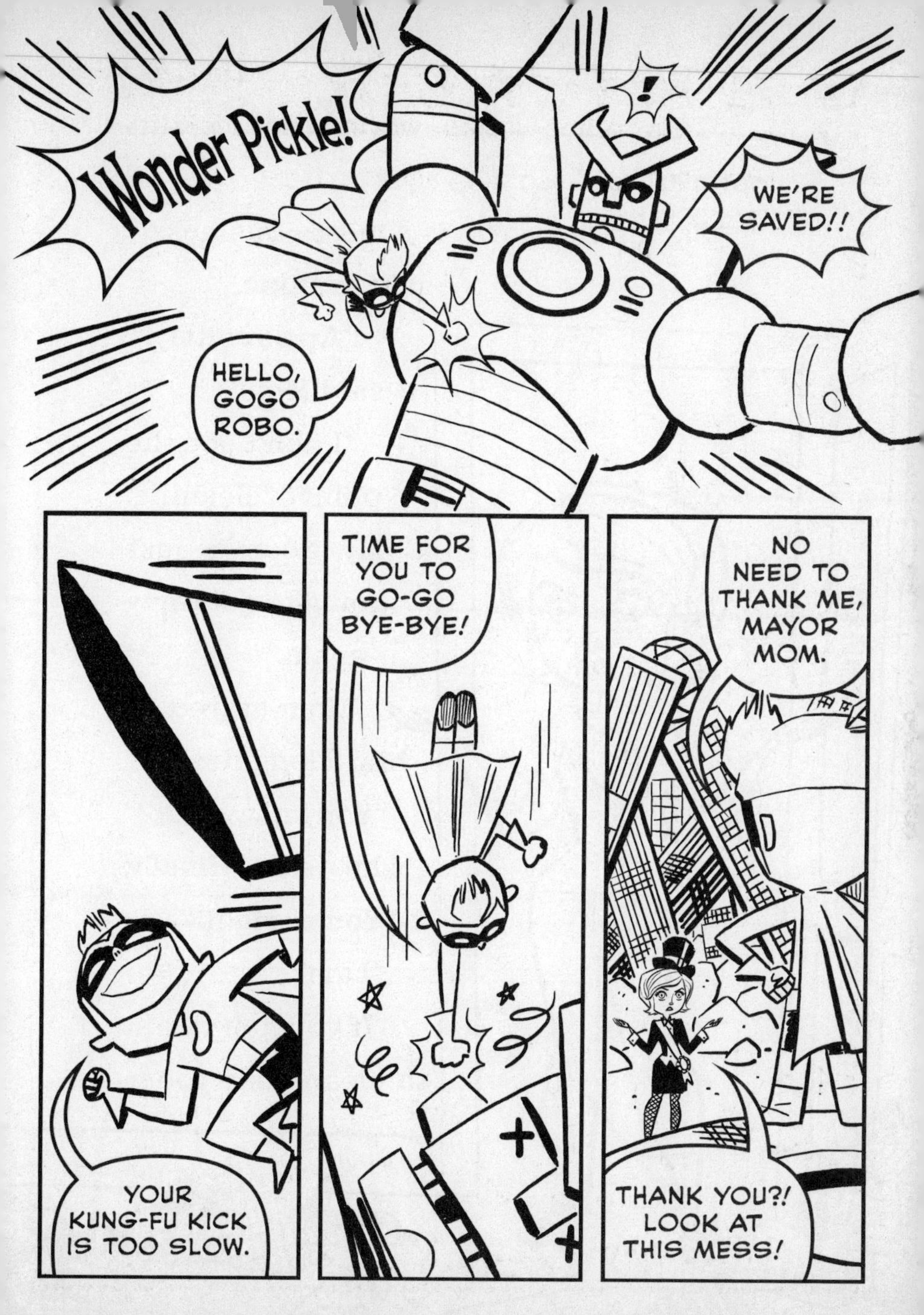
Wonder Pickle!
!
WE'RE SAVED!!
HELLO, GOGO ROBO.
YOUR KUNG-FU KICK IS TOO SLOW.
TIME FOR YOU TO GO-GO BYE-BYE!
NO NEED TO THANK ME, MAYOR MOM.
THANK YOU?! LOOK AT THIS MESS!

"This place looks worse than it did before," said Mom.

"Saving the world is a messy business," said Frankie.

"Apparently," said Mom.

"I don't see the point of cleaning. My room's just going to get dirty again."

Mom stared at him a long time.

"You know what?" she said finally. "You're right."

"I am?"

"If you don't want to clean your room,

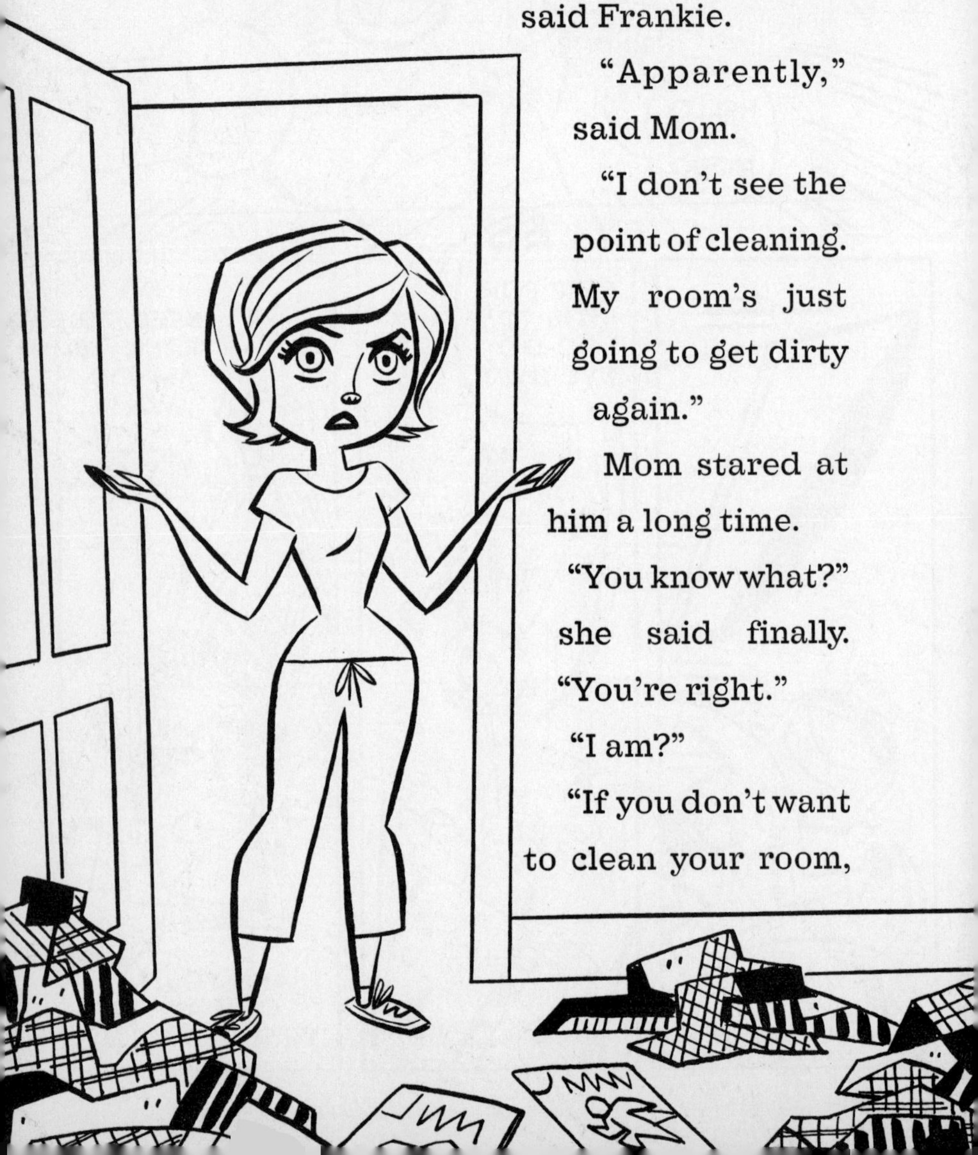

you don't have to."

"I don't?" Frankie couldn't believe his ears.

"Nope. This is your space. Do with it what you want."

"Really?"

"Really." Frankie's mom turned to leave but stopped at the door. "There is one catch," she said. "Whatever happens, you have to deal with the consequences."

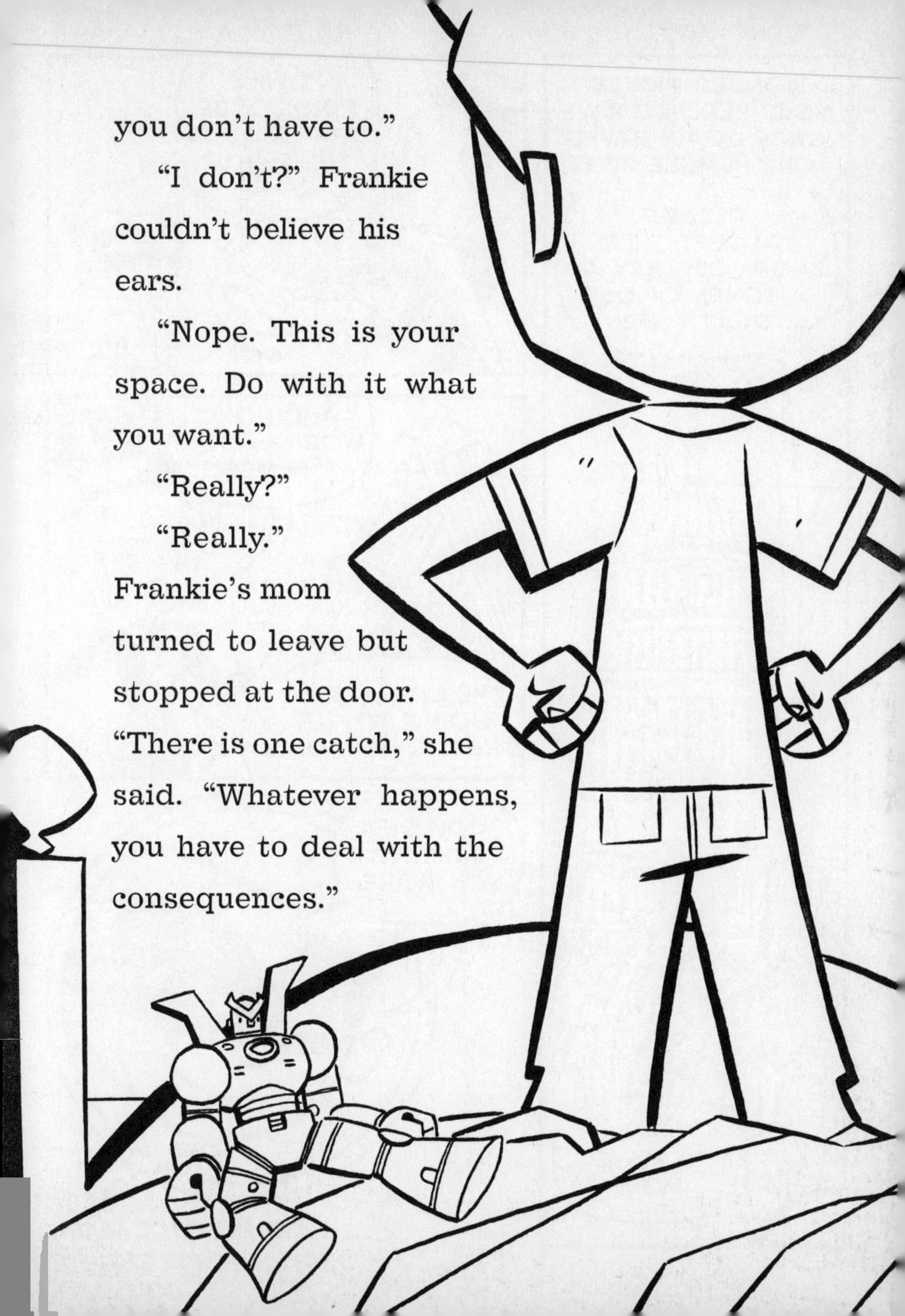

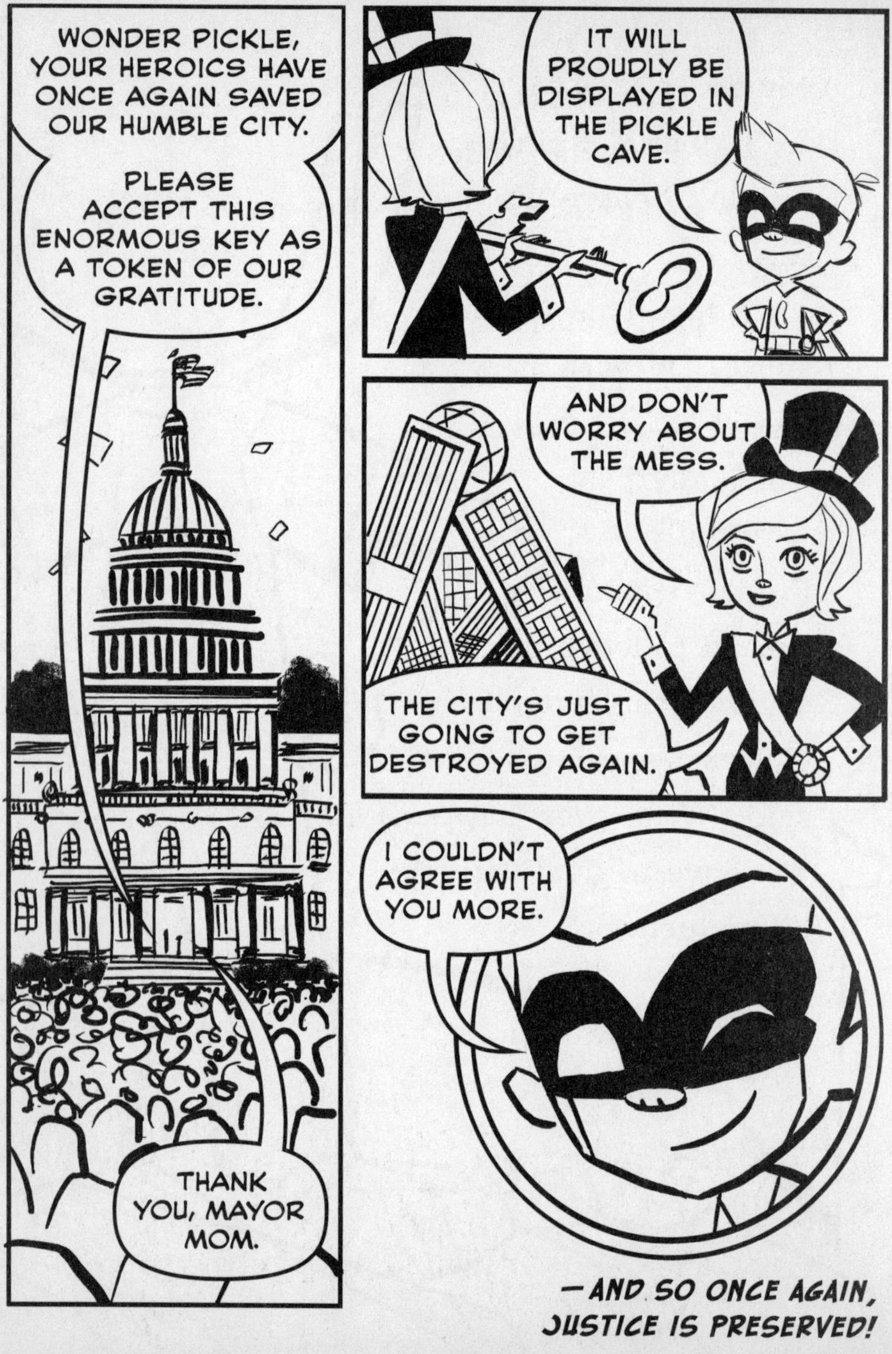
WONDER PICKLE, YOUR HEROICS HAVE ONCE AGAIN SAVED OUR HUMBLE CITY.
PLEASE ACCEPT THIS ENORMOUS KEY AS A TOKEN OF OUR GRATITUDE.
THANK YOU, MAYOR MOM.
IT WILL PROUDLY BE DISPLAYED IN THE PICKLE CAVE.
AND DON'T WORRY ABOUT THE MESS.
THE CITY'S JUST GOING TO GET DESTROYED AGAIN.
I COULDN'T AGREE WITH YOU MORE.
—AND SO ONCE AGAIN, JUSTICE IS PRESERVED!

“I can definitely handle those consequences,” said Frankie.

He laid on the floor of his room making snow angels in the clutter. The clutter he never had to clean up again.

Justice had been preserved.

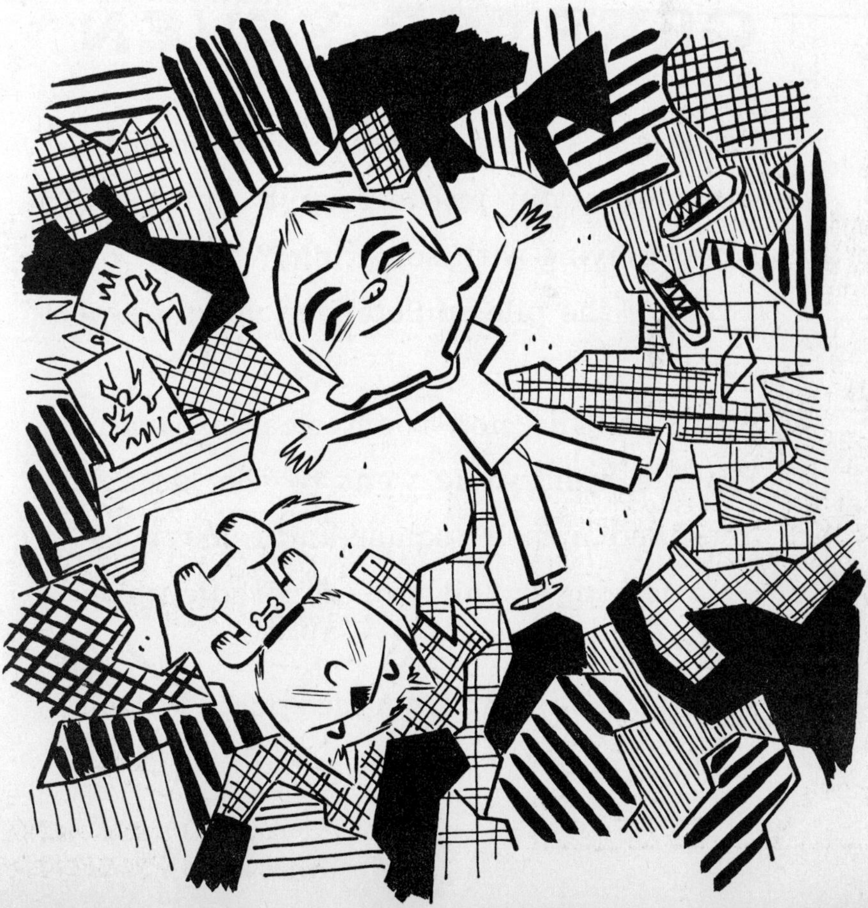

CHAPTER SEVEN

Frankie was living on cloud swine. No more worrying about where to put stuff. Finished playing with something? Toss it on a pile. If the pile spilled over, start a new one.

All of this non-room cleaning made Frankie hungry. He went to the kitchen and fixed himself a salami-and-relish sandwich, leaving a snail trail of ingredients on the counter.

Piper looked up from the sports section

of the newspaper. "You better not leave any crumbs," she said. "Mom just cleaned in here."

"I'm not worried," said Frankie. "We have an understanding."

"What's all this?!" Mom shouted as she walked into the kitchen.

Frankie jumped. "But I thought . . ."

"Just because you can make a mess in your room, doesn't mean you can destroy

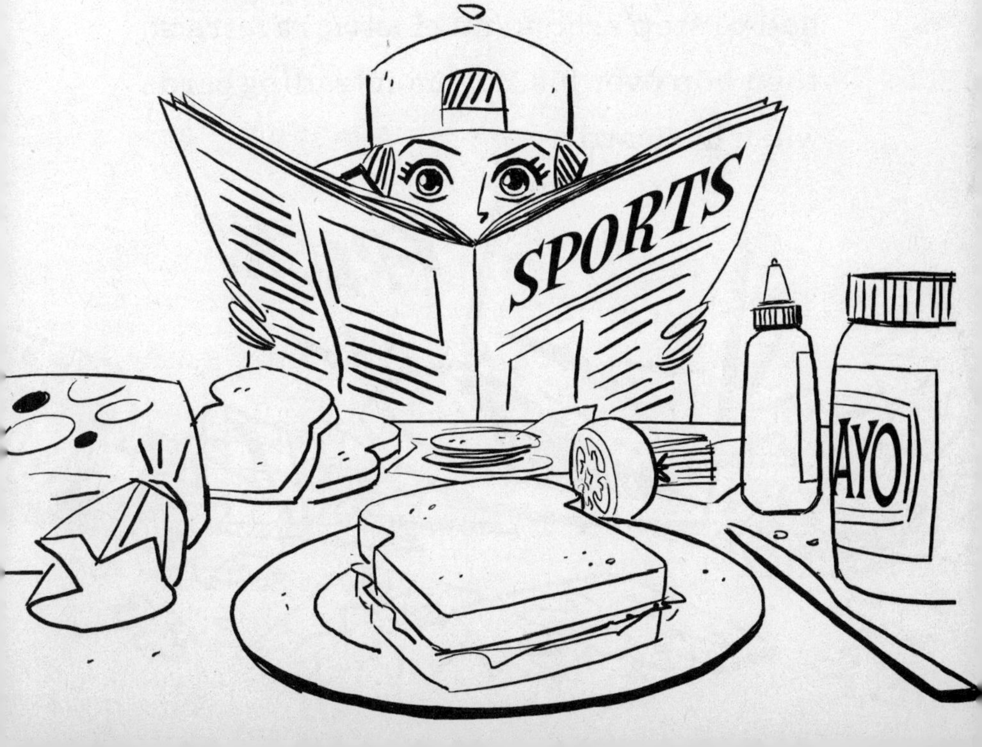
SPORTS
AYO

the rest of the house," said Mom. "Put all of this food away before it spoils."

"Fine," said Frankie.

"And you better not leave any crumbs," said Mom.

"Told you so," said Piper.

Frankie put everything away. He'd go eat his sandwich in his room—the one place he was free to leave crumbs.

On the way over to his bed, Frankie had to step around an electric racetrack, then hop over his Yugimon trading cards when he heard a—

KRACK!

He froze, afraid to look down. *It's going to be okay*, he told himself. Probably just a pretzel or a really big cockroach or . . .

"It's Hammerin' Time," the thing under his foot said.

Frankie gasped, dropping his salami-and-relish sandwich. He had stepped on GoGo Robo! And his bionic leg with the Battle-Action Kung-Fu Kick™ was broken!!

CHAPTER EIGHT

Trying not to panic, Frankie carefully picked up his wounded warrior. The leg dangled by a sliver of metal-colored plastic. There was only one person who would know how to save him.

Frankie spun around, slipping on a Yugimon card. Somehow he stayed on his feet, knocking over a pyramid of empty juice boxes in the process. He ran past Piper's room. She was busy arranging her cleats according to season.

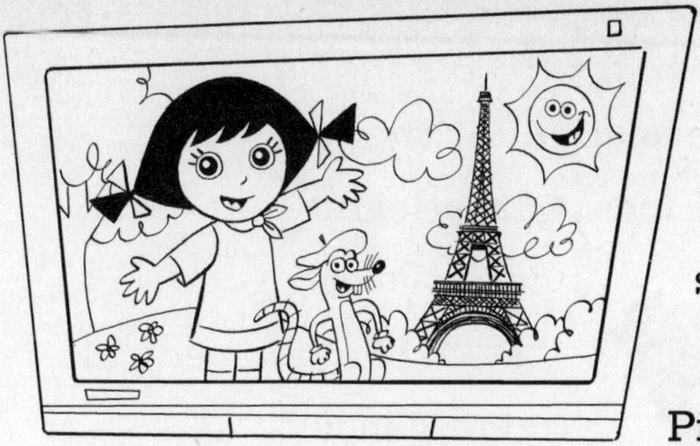

"Have you seen Dad?" said Frankie.

"Nope," said Piper.

Mom passed Frankie in the hallway. "Did you need something?" she said. Frankie hid GoGo Robo behind his back. If he couldn't deal with this consequence himself, he'd have to go back to cleaning his room.

"Nothing in particular," he said. "You know, guy stuff."

"Okay." Mom continued on her way.

Frankie went downstairs. Lucy sat in her play yard watching her favorite TV show, *Avril the Traveler.*

"Bonjour, mes amis!" said the animated girl with the melon-shaped head. "Let's travel together!" No sign of Dad

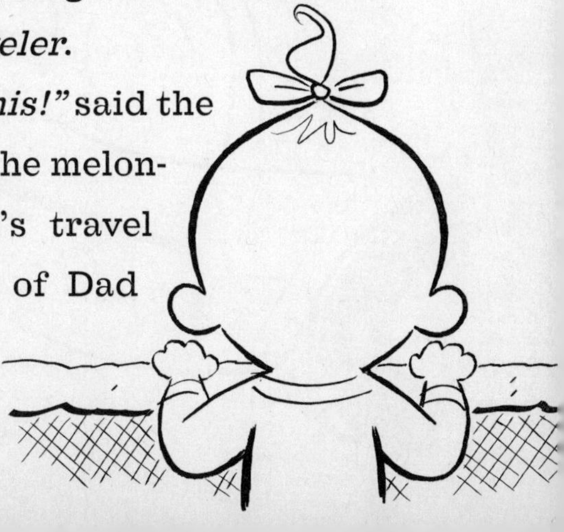

here. Frankie headed for the garage.

A pair of legs was sticking out from under the car.

"Dad! I have a medical emergency!"

Frankie's dad slid out from under the car so fast, he banged his head on the bumper—

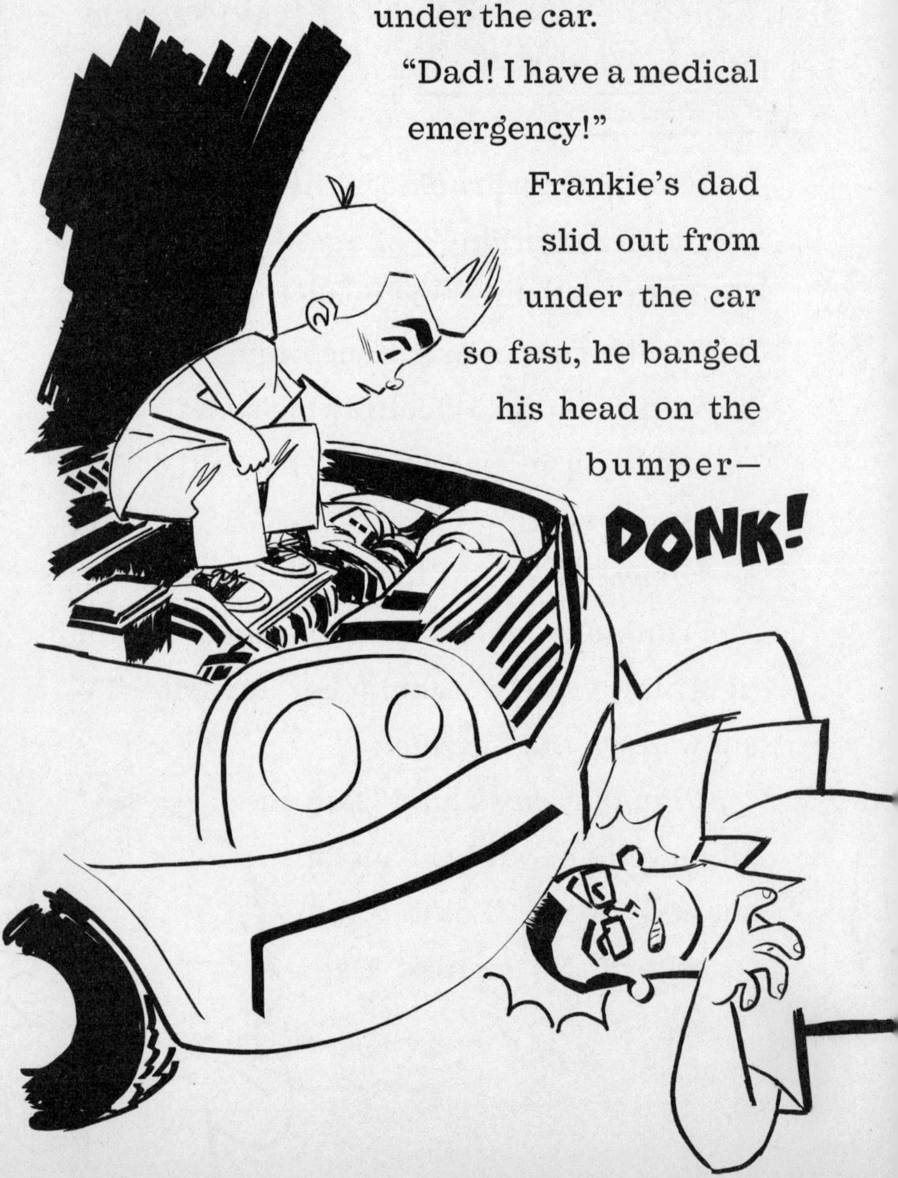
DONK!

"What happened? Are you okay? Do you still have all your fingers?"

"I'm fine," said Frankie. "But GoGo Robo is in critical condition."

"Geez," said Dad, rubbing his forehead. "Wish I could help. But you know the rules."

Frankie started to pout.

"Now, if it had happened to *my* robot action figure," Dad continued, "some epoxy glue would fix it."

"Thanks, Dad."

Frankie found the glue and went back to the kitchen to scrub in for surgery.

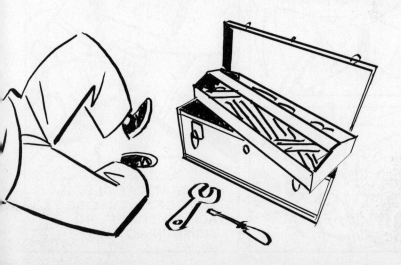

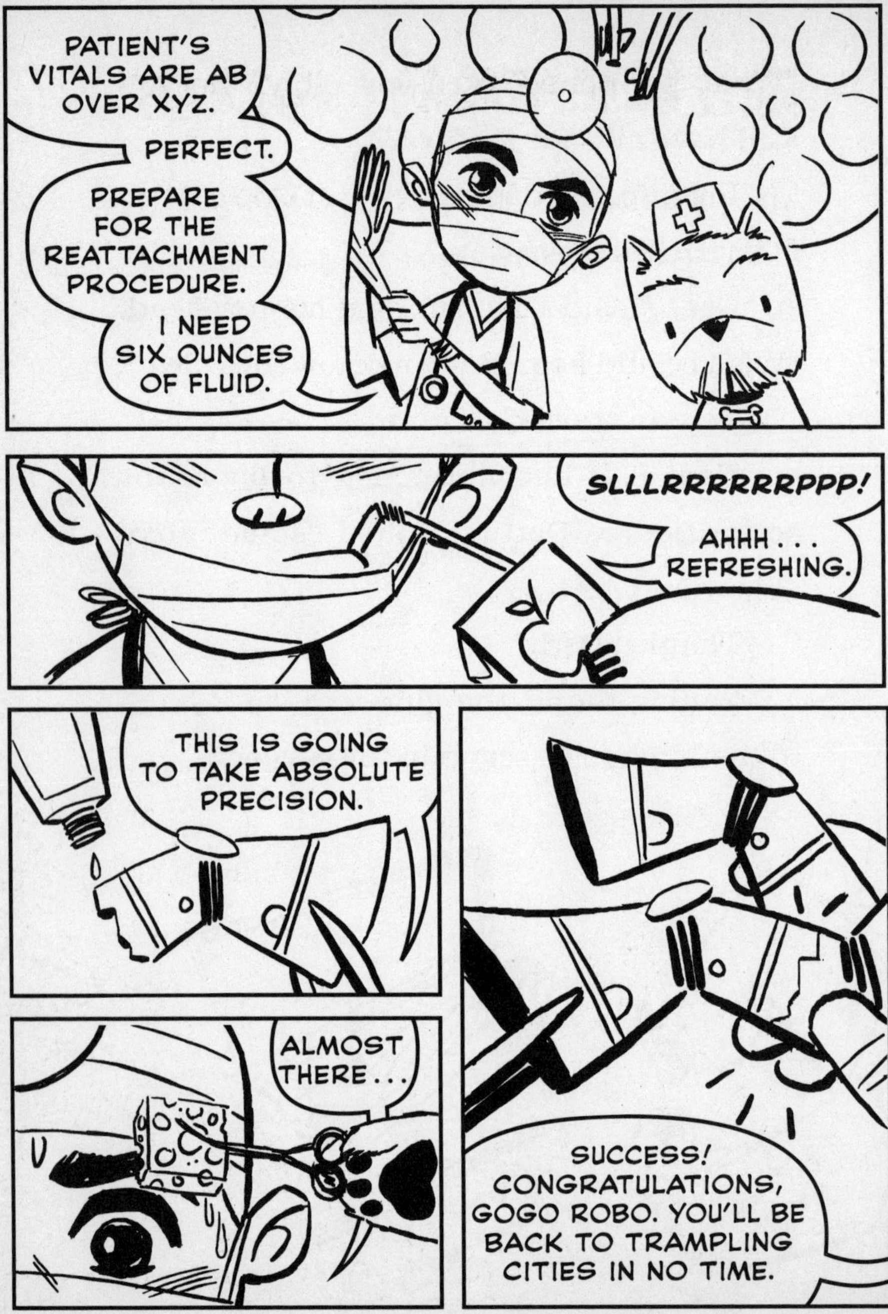
PATIENT'S VITALS ARE AB OVER XYZ.
PERFECT.
PREPARE FOR THE REATTACHMENT PROCEDURE.
I NEED SIX OUNCES OF FLUID.
SLLLRRRRRRPPP!
AHHH . . . REFRESHING.
THIS IS GOING TO TAKE ABSOLUTE PRECISION.
ALMOST THERE . . .
SUCCESS! CONGRATULATIONS, GOGO ROBO. YOU'LL BE BACK TO TRAMPLING CITIES IN NO TIME.

CHAPTER NINE

After the close call with GoGo Robo, Frankie knew there was no consequence he couldn't handle. He would NEVER have to clean his room again.

As the days passed, the Dryer Sheet Fairy stopped visiting. Frankie didn't mind. The mounds of clothes on the floor added extra cushion for when he and Argyle wrestled.

The clutter started to multiply. Piles formed on top of piles. Heaps became mountains.

The Pickle Cave was turning into the Pickle Pit.

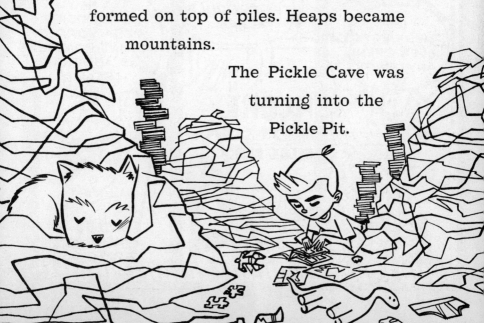

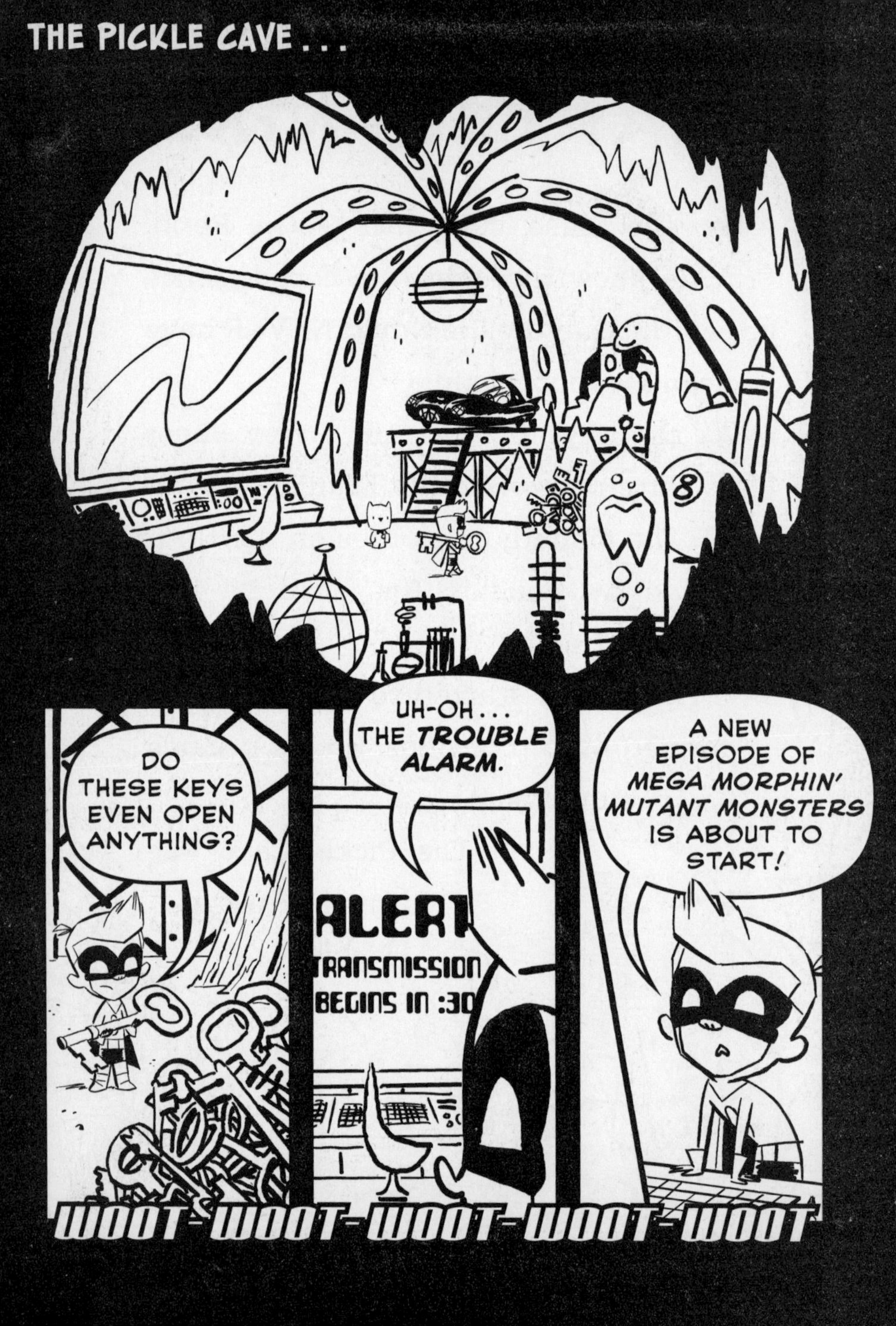
THE PICKLE CAVE . . .
DO THESE KEYS EVEN OPEN ANYTHING?
UH-OH . . . THE *TROUBLE ALARM.*
ALERT
TRANSMISSION
BEGINS IN :30
A NEW EPISODE OF *MEGA MORPHIN' MUTANT MONSTERS* IS ABOUT TO START!
WOOT-WOOT-WOOT-WOOT-WOOT

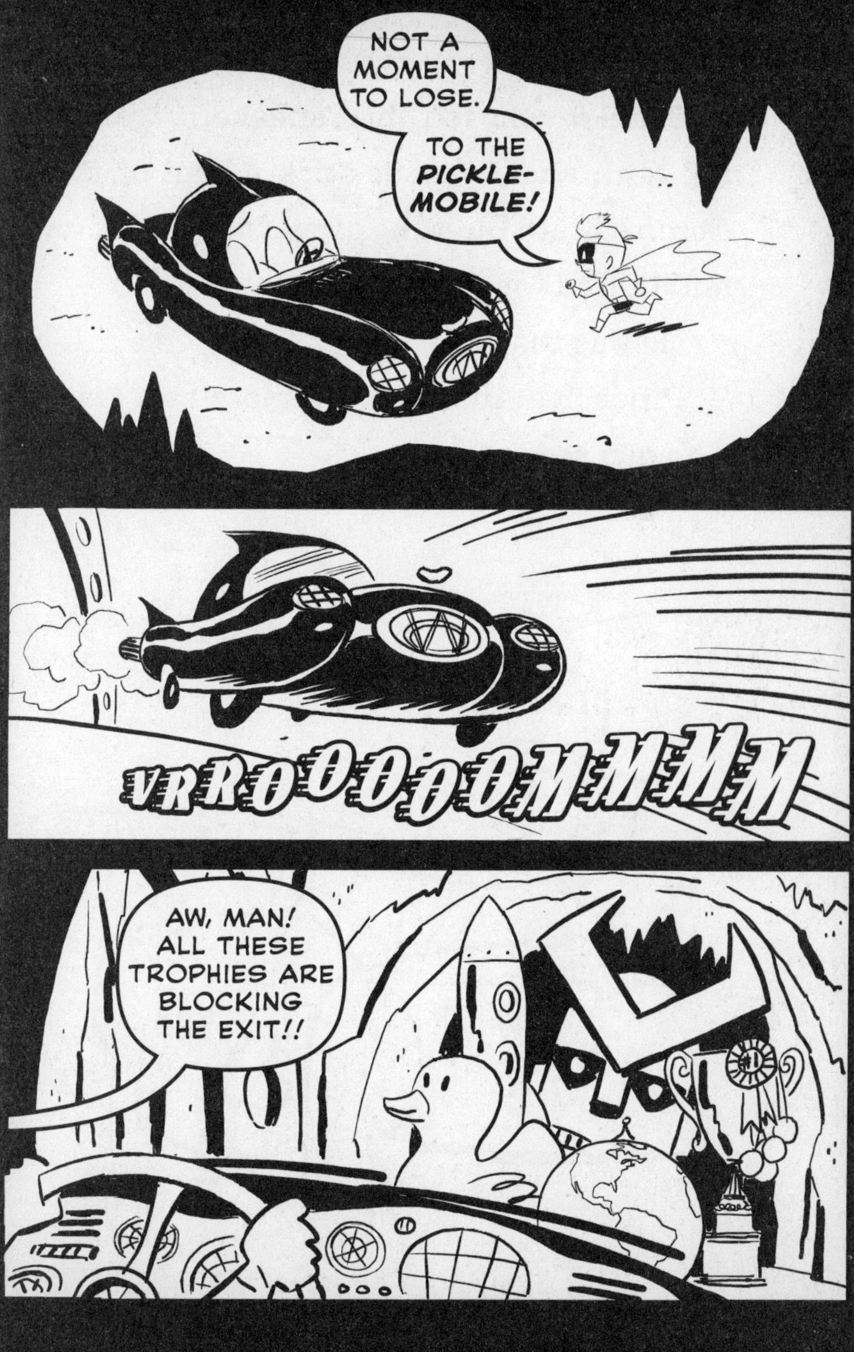
NOT A MOMENT TO LOSE.
TO THE PICKLE-MOBILE!
VRROOOOOOMMMMM
AW, MAN! ALL THESE TROPHIES ARE BLOCKING THE EXIT!!

Frankie shoved his sneakers, camping tent, and Popsicle-stick model of the Empire State Building away from the door and bolted for the TV room.

He was too late.

Piper beat him to the remote by a fraction of a second.

CHAPTER TEN

"My show's about to start!" said Frankie.

Piper was more concerned about his outfit.

"What are you wearing??" she said.

"Duh. Clothes," said Frankie. "Pass the remote."

"You look like your closet barfed on you."

"This is the only clean stuff I have," said Frankie. Which was true, although his shirt had kind of a beefy aroma. "I don't have time for this. My show is going to start."

"I was here first."

"DAAAADDD!"

Dad came over to referee.

"Sorry, Champ. Piper was here first. You can record your show and watch it when she's done."

Twenty-three minutes of sports highlights from around the globe later, Frankie finally got his turn.

CHAPTER ELEVEN

Soon Frankie added himself to that list of things he wasn't cleaning. Why bathe when you're just going to get dirty again? Of course, he failed to take into account how grimy you get playing G.I. JIM in the mulch.

Every Friday night was Family Fun Night, a time when the Piccolini family gathered at the kitchen table. They'd play board games, share stories, and enjoy some of Dad's freshly baked cookies. Frankie couldn't understand why tonight

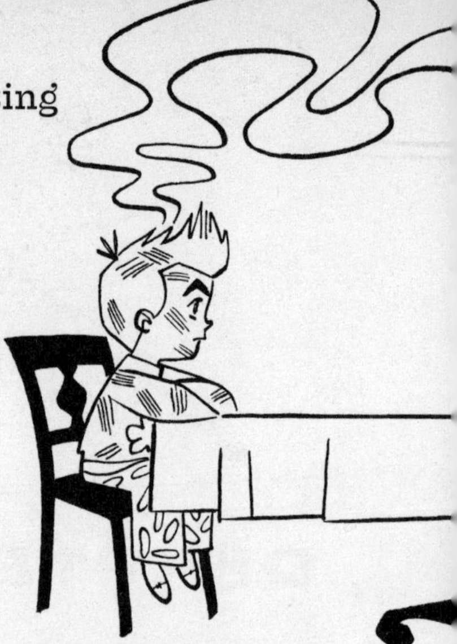

everyone insisted on sitting as far away from him as possible.

"So, Frankie, how are things working out with your room?" said Dad, trying to breathe through only his mouth.

"Great," said Frankie.

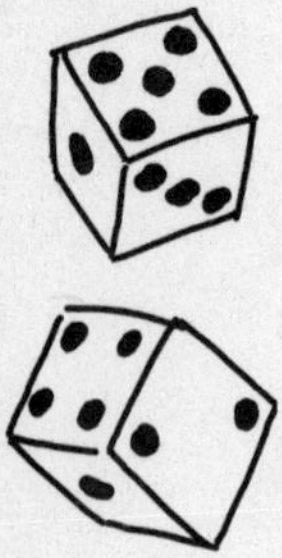

"As long as you're not downwind," said Piper.

Mom gave her The Look. The one that freezes water.

"Seriously, Mom. You're going to have to change his name to Stankie."

"We all have a natural aroma," said Frankie.

"Yours happens to be ripe garbage."

"That's enough, Piper." Mom lit a few scented candles. Dad put out a plate of

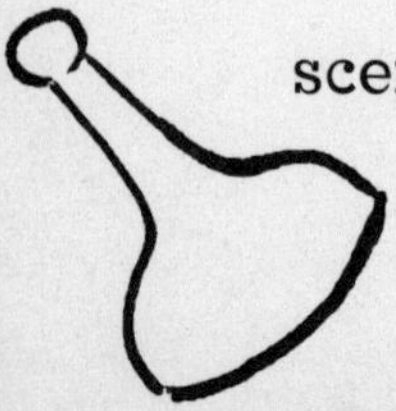

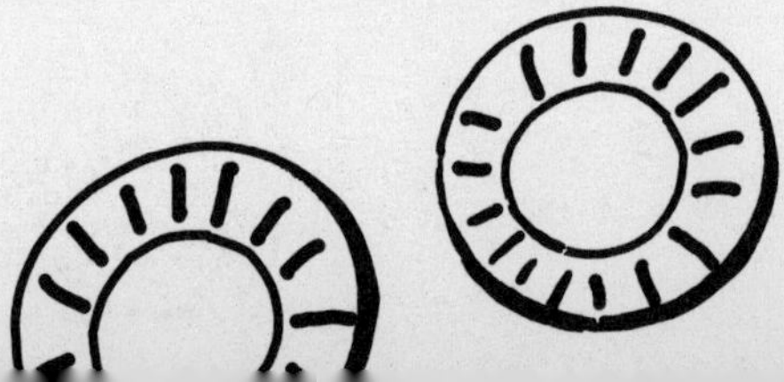

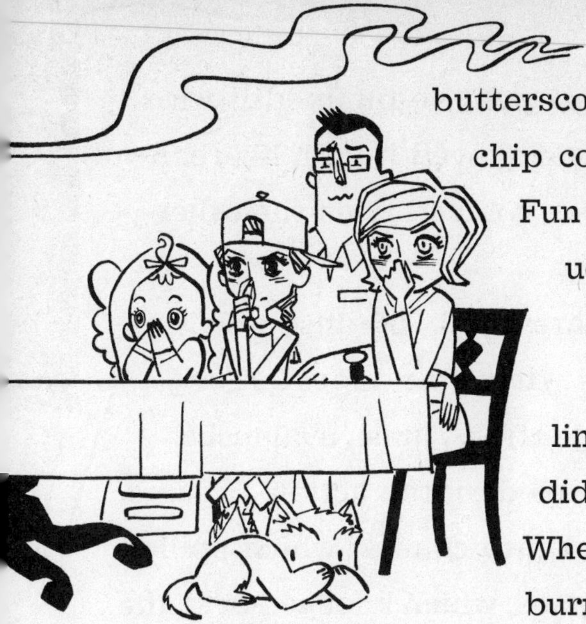

butterscotch chocolate chip cookies. Family Fun Night continued as usual. Almost.

As the night lingered on, so did the stench. When the candles burned out, Dad snuck an air freshener under Frankie's chair. That just made the room smell like a landfill in the middle of a pine forest.

One by one, everyone found an excuse to go to sleep early. Piper even threw her last turn—breaking her seven-game winning streak.

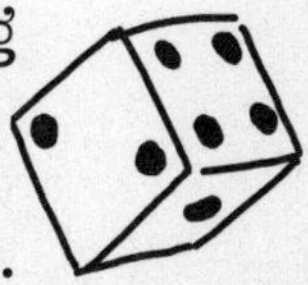

Before too long, Frankie was all alone. He figured he might as well go to bed too. But when he tried to get into his room, the

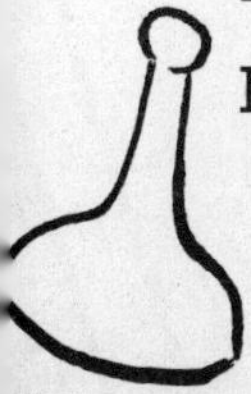

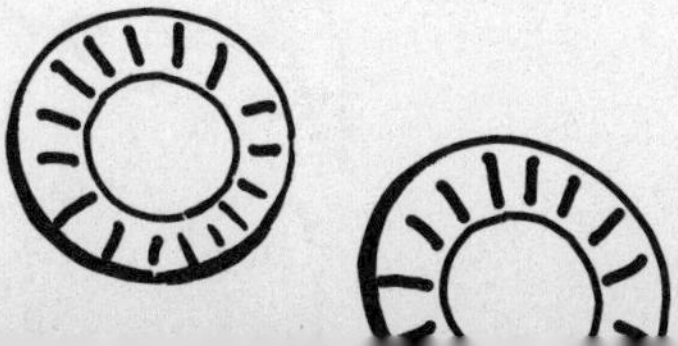

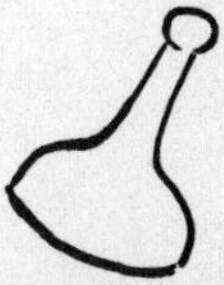

door wouldn't open. He bumped it with his shoulder. He shoved it with his rear. No good. It was jammed from the other side.

Frankie threw all of his weight into it. This time the door swung open, setting off a junk avalanche. Clothing tumbled into action figures, which toppled into comics, which spilled into board games, which knocked over the trash can.

The floor was completely covered in spillage.

Wading through the mess, Frankie was just happy nothing had landed on him.

Argyle stayed in the doorway.

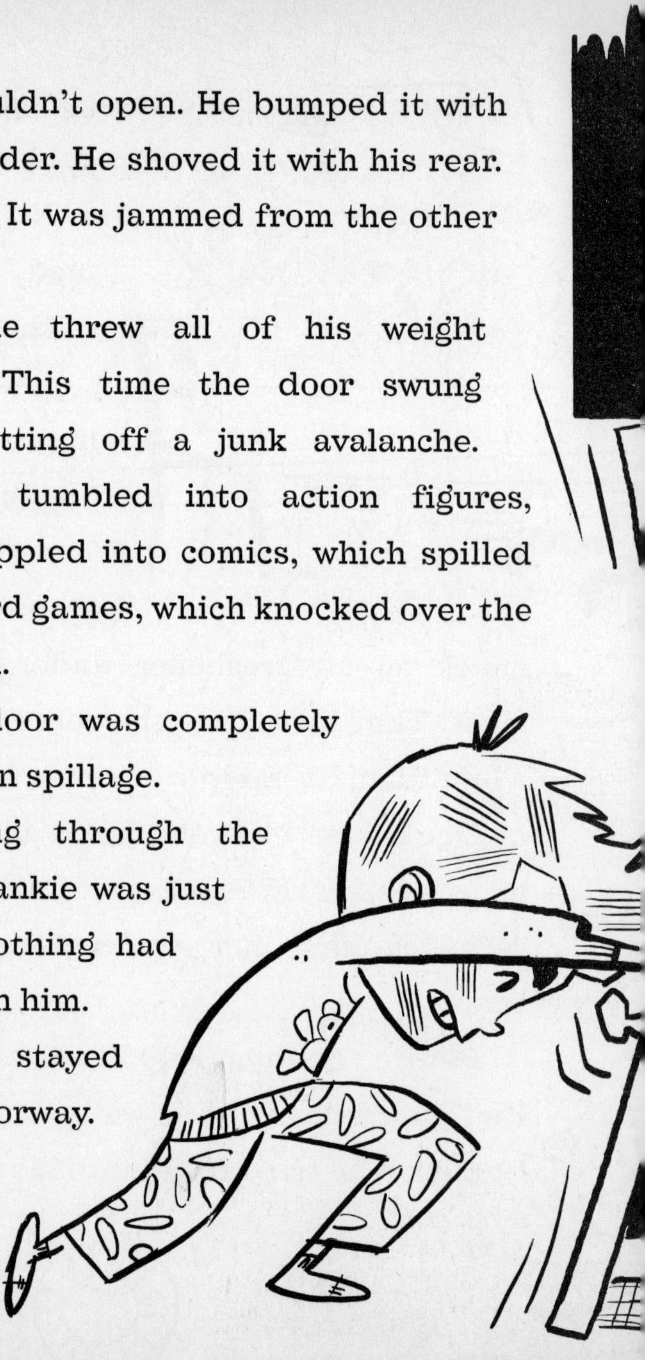

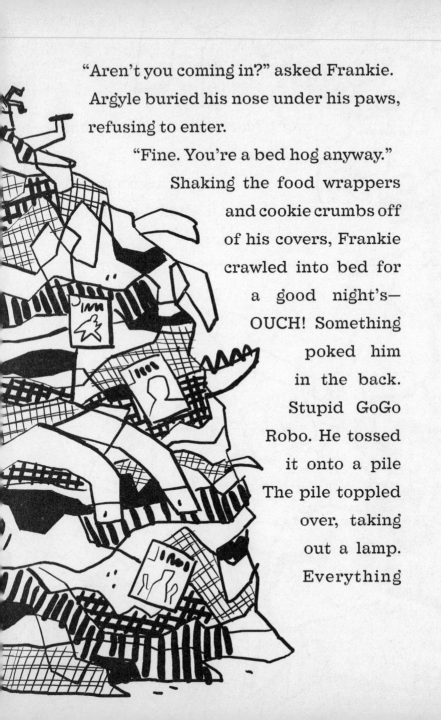

"Aren't you coming in?" asked Frankie. Argyle buried his nose under his paws, refusing to enter.

"Fine. You're a bed hog anyway." Shaking the food wrappers and cookie crumbs off of his covers, Frankie crawled into bed for a good night's— OUCH! Something poked him in the back. Stupid GoGo Robo. He tossed it onto a pile The pile toppled over, taking out a lamp. Everything

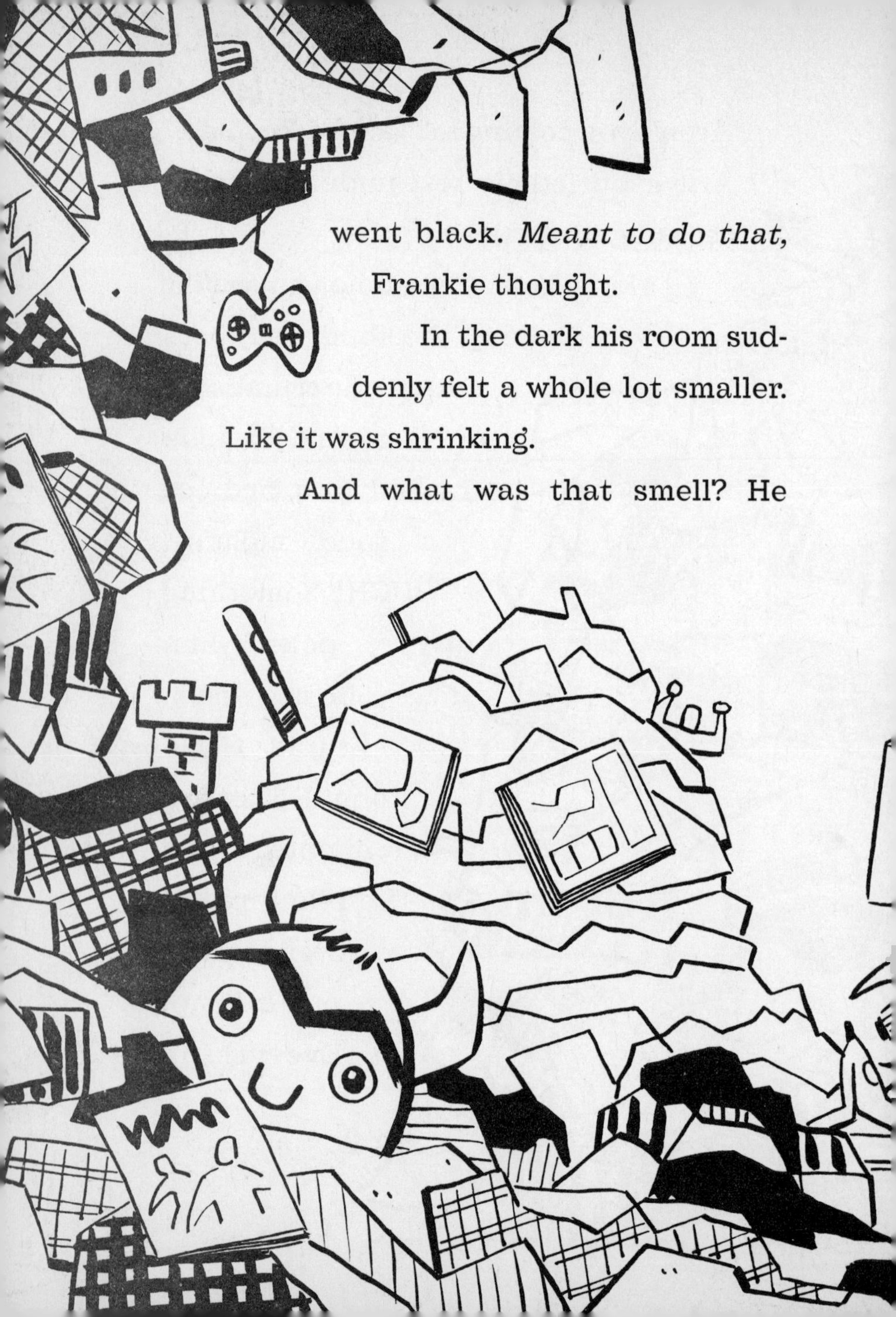

went black. *Meant to do that,* Frankie thought.

In the dark his room suddenly felt a whole lot smaller. Like it was shrinking.

And what was that smell? He

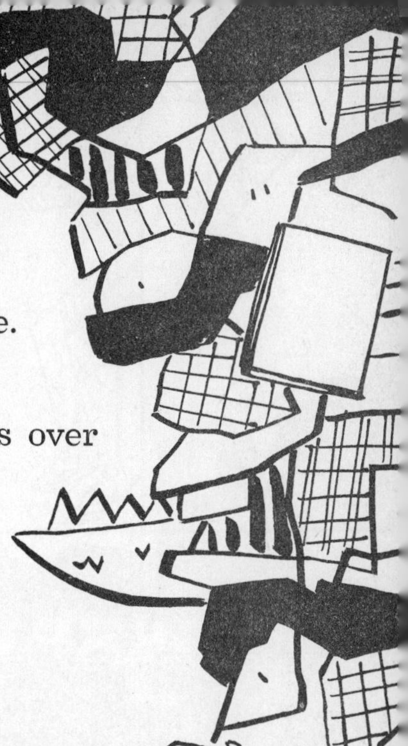

sniffed his armpit.

Nope. It was something else. Something awful.

Frankie pulled the covers over his head and tried not to think about it.

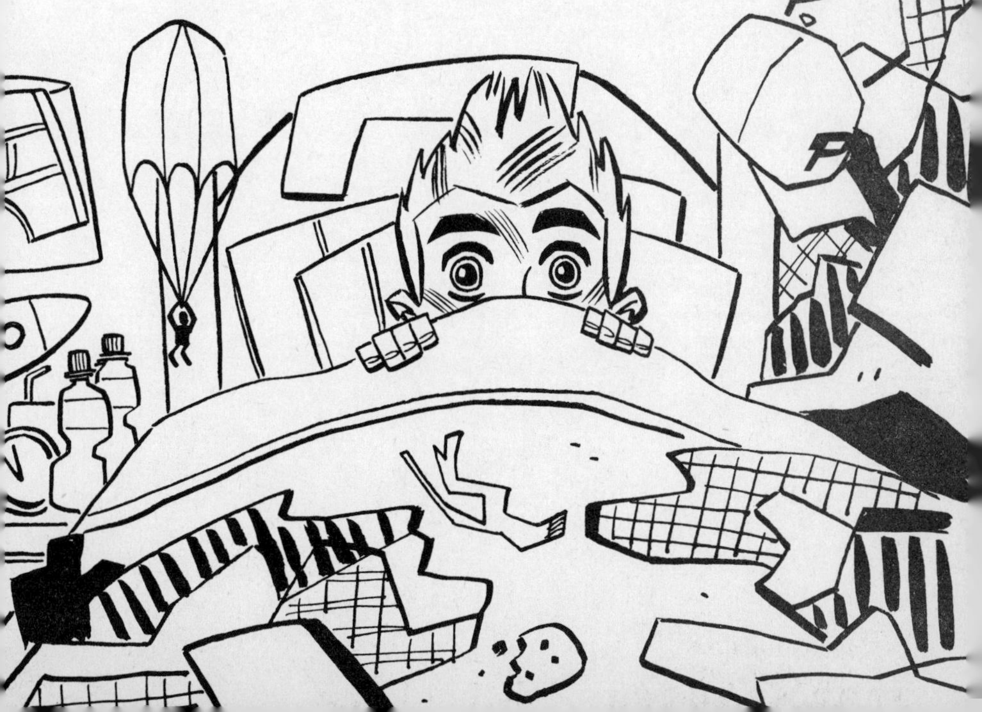

CHAPTER TWELVE

Something shook Frankie awake. At first he thought it was an earthquake. But he must have dreamed it. Real or not, he couldn't fall back to sleep.

Maybe a drink of water would help. Frankie swung his legs over the side of his bed and hopped down.

But he didn't land on the floor. He went right through it.

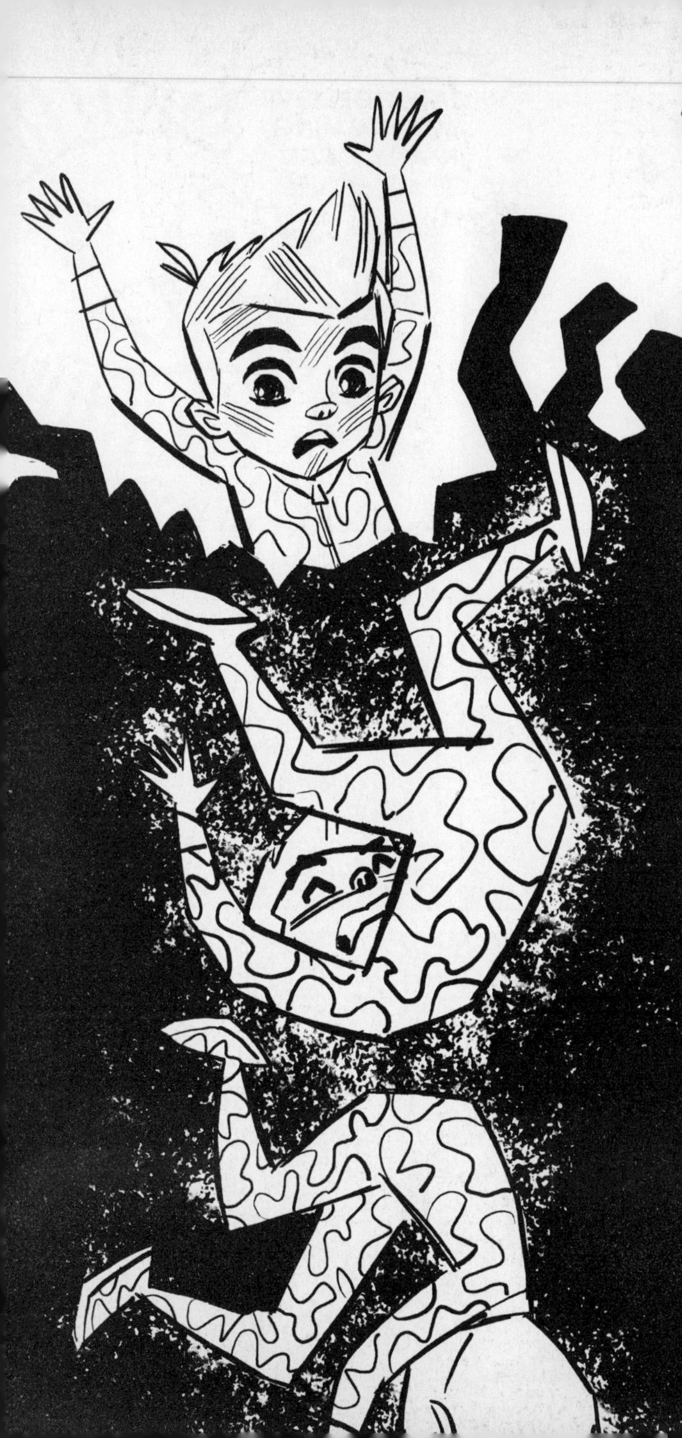

Deeper
and
deeper
he fell
into a
bottomless
pit of
messiness.

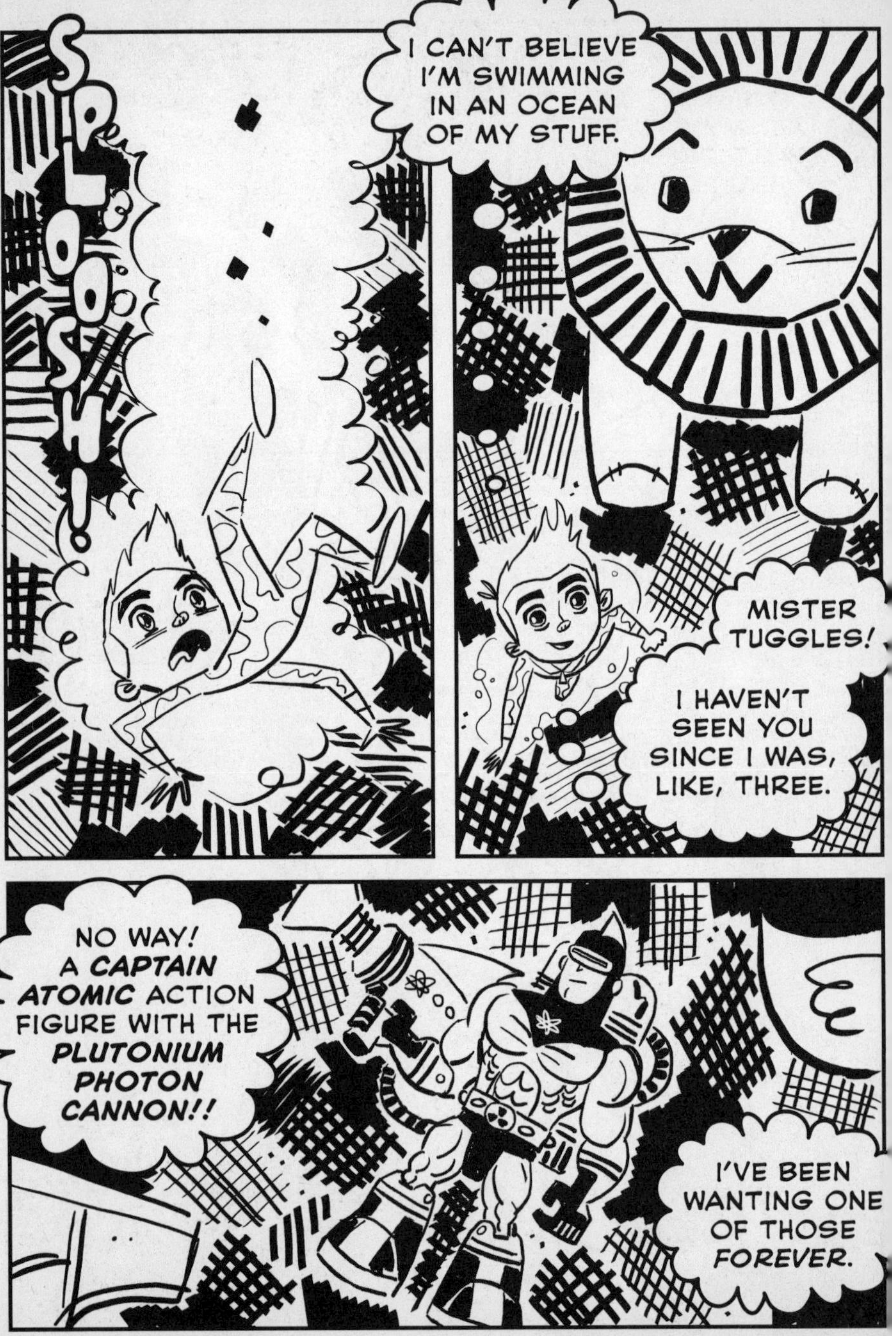
SPLOOSH!
I CAN'T BELIEVE I'M SWIMMING IN AN OCEAN OF MY STUFF.
MISTER TUGGLES!
I HAVEN'T SEEN YOU SINCE I WAS, LIKE, THREE.
NO WAY! A *CAPTAIN ATOMIC* ACTION FIGURE WITH THE *PLUTONIUM PHOTON CANNON!!*
I'VE BEEN WANTING ONE OF THOSE *FOREVER.*

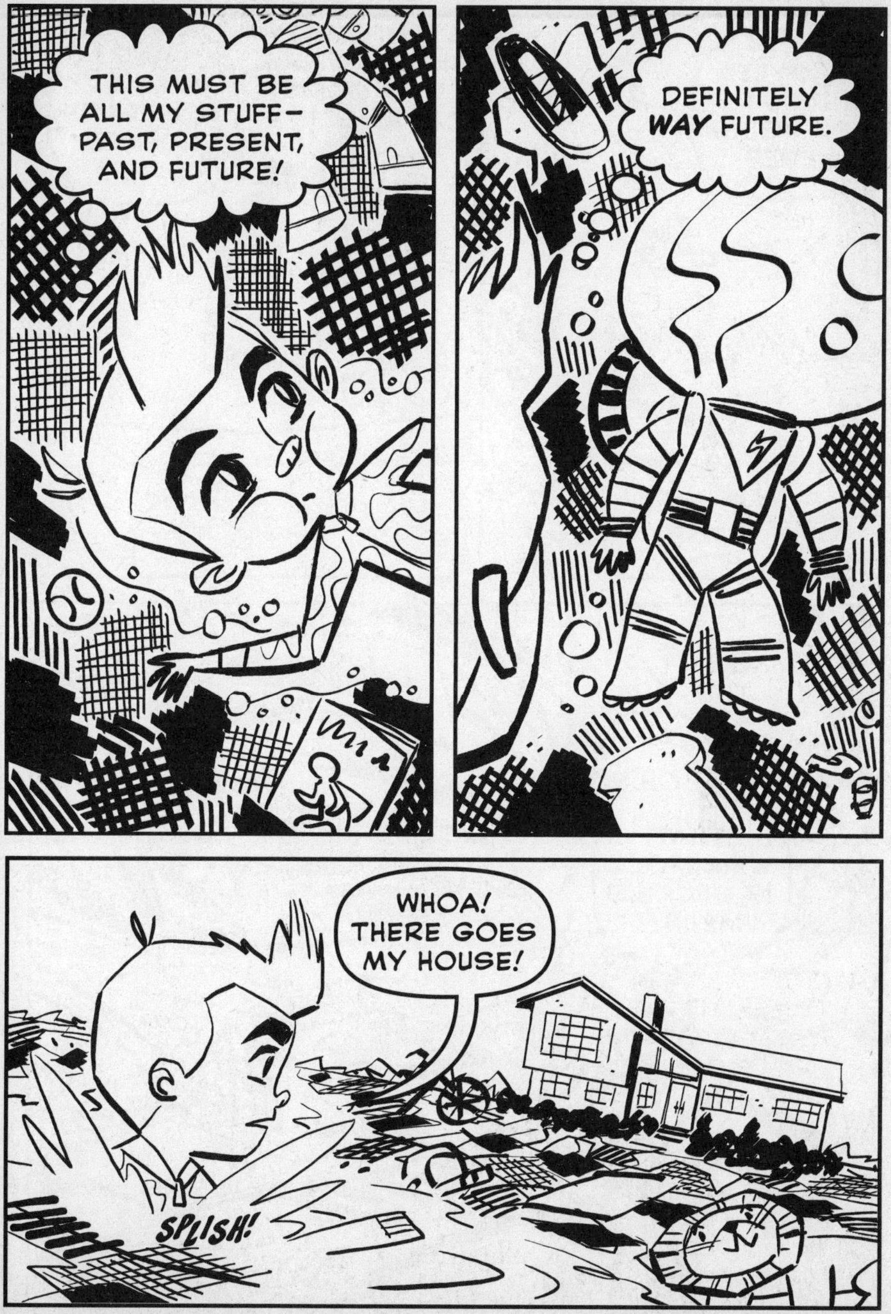
THIS MUST BE ALL MY STUFF–PAST, PRESENT, AND FUTURE!
DEFINITELY *WAY* FUTURE.
WHOA! THERE GOES MY HOUSE!
SPLISH!

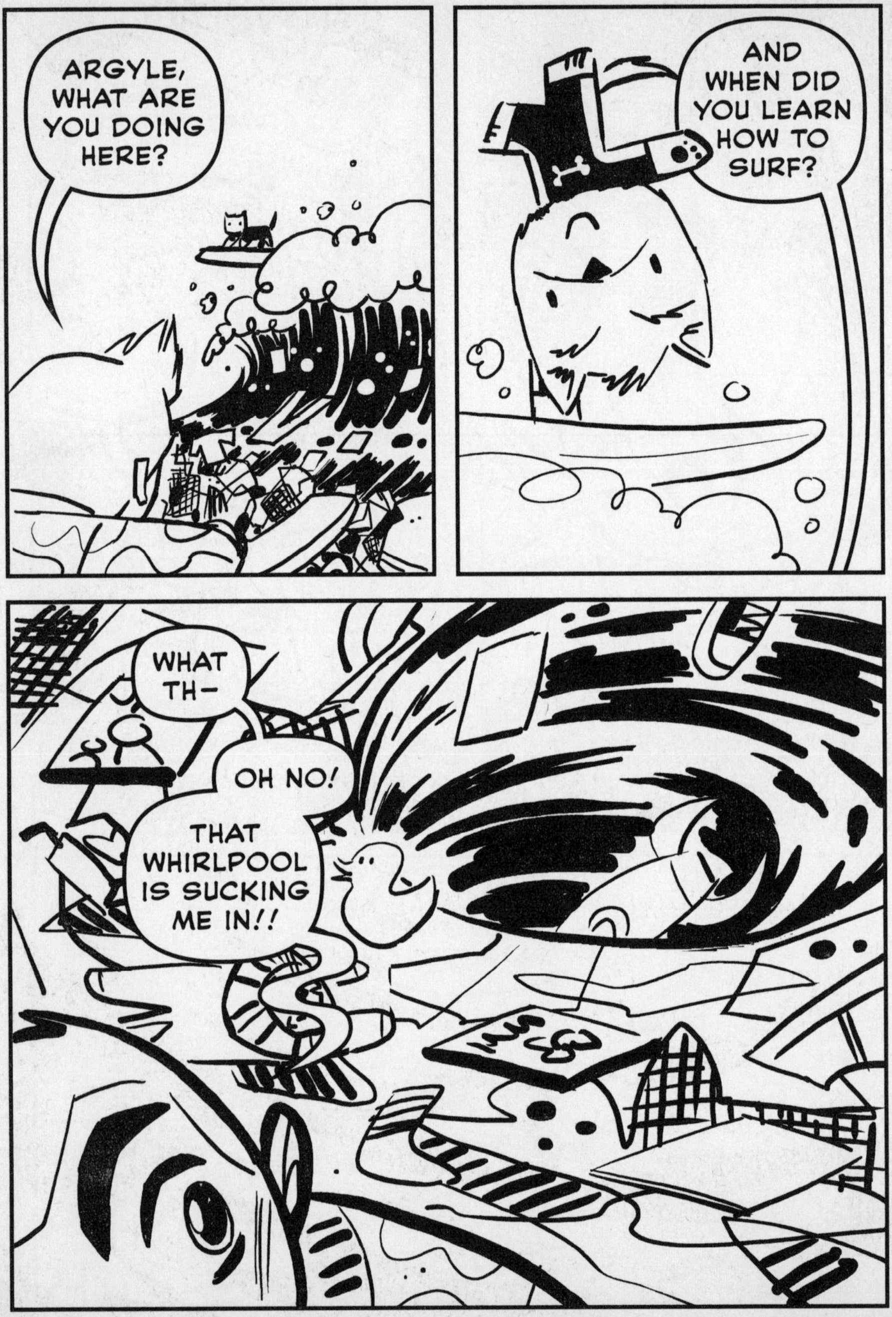
ARGYLE, WHAT ARE YOU DOING HERE?
AND WHEN DID YOU LEARN HOW TO SURF?
WHAT TH—
OH NO!
THAT WHIRLPOOL IS SUCKING ME IN!!

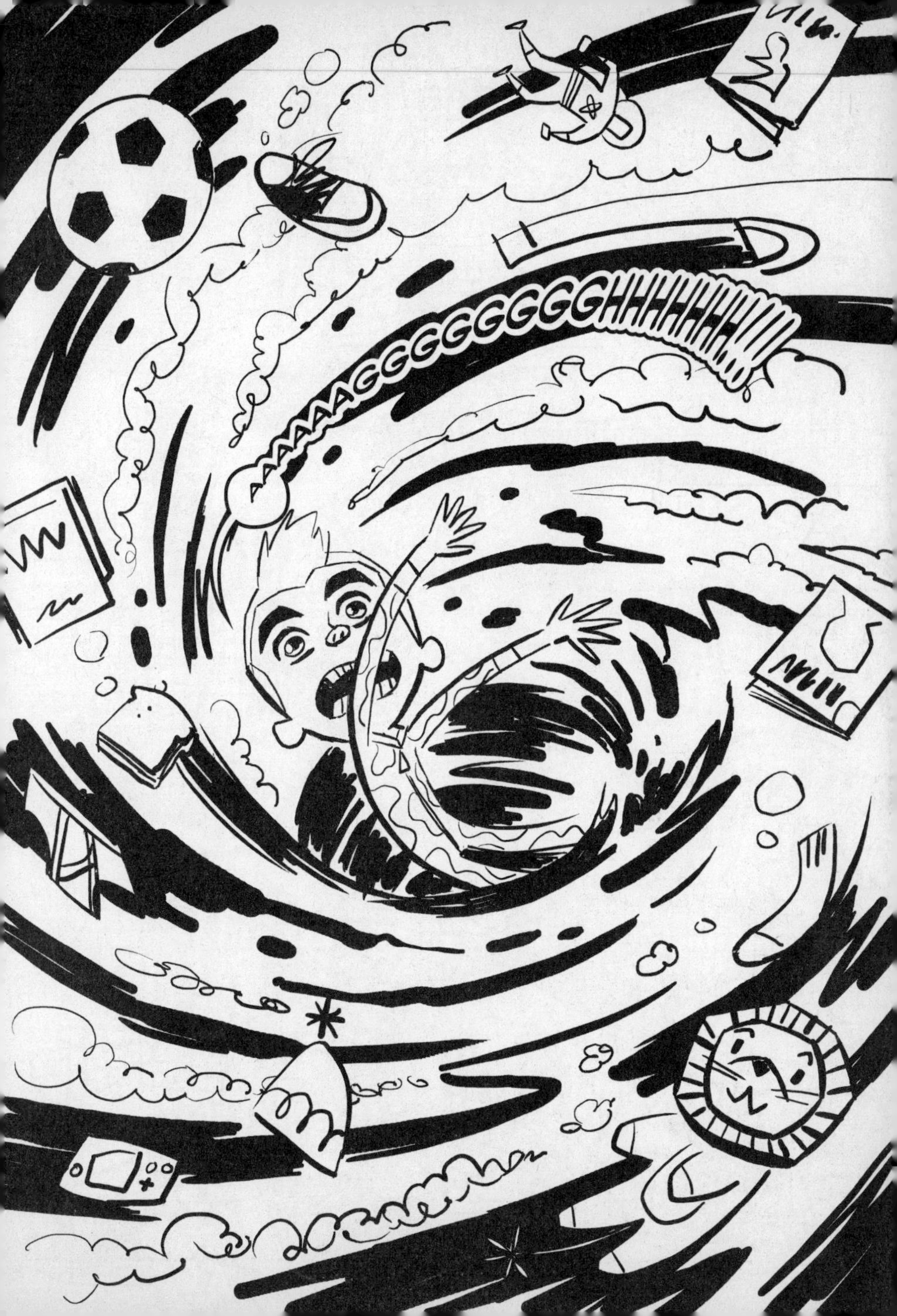
AAAAAAAGGGGGGGGHHHHHHH!!!!

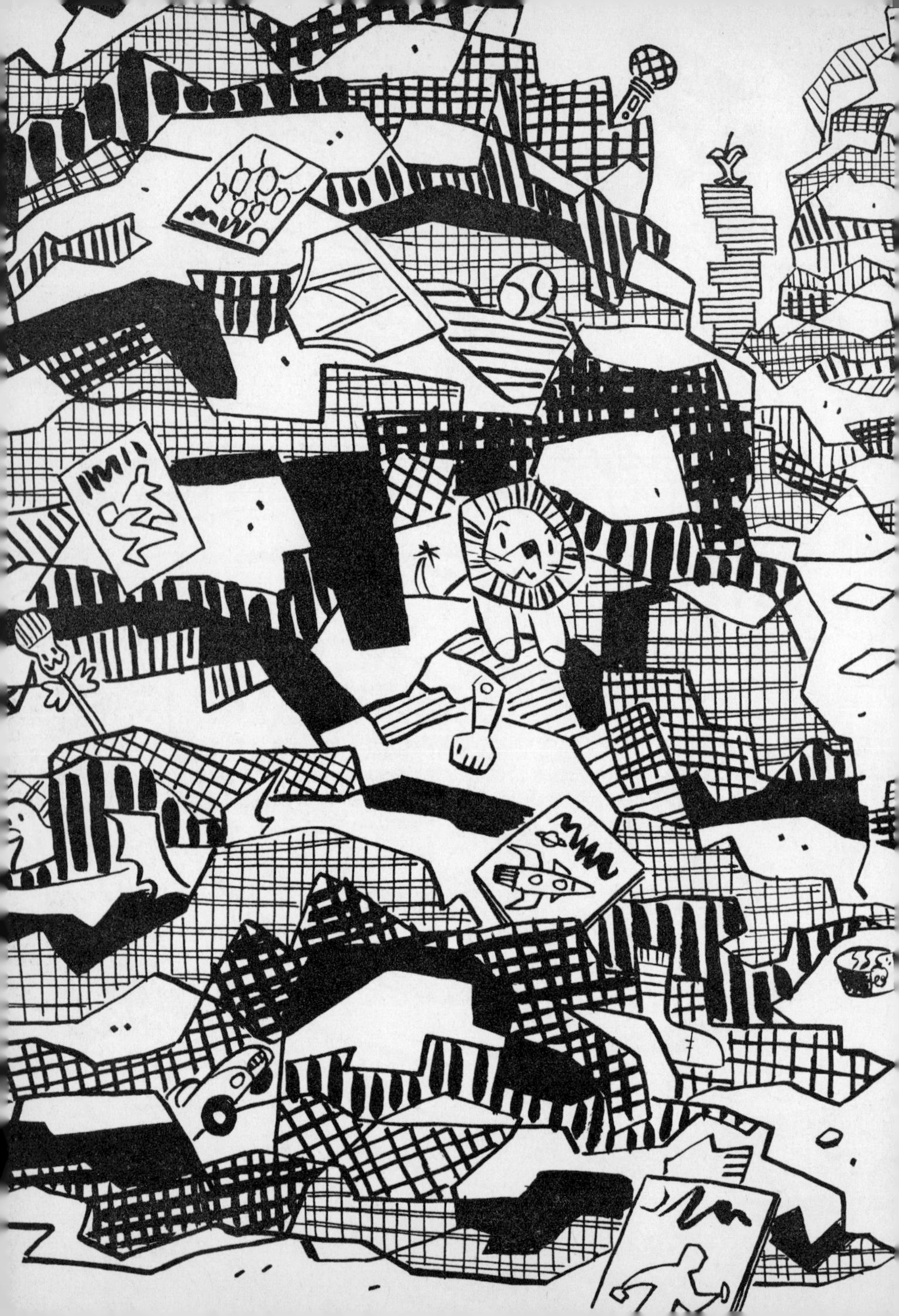

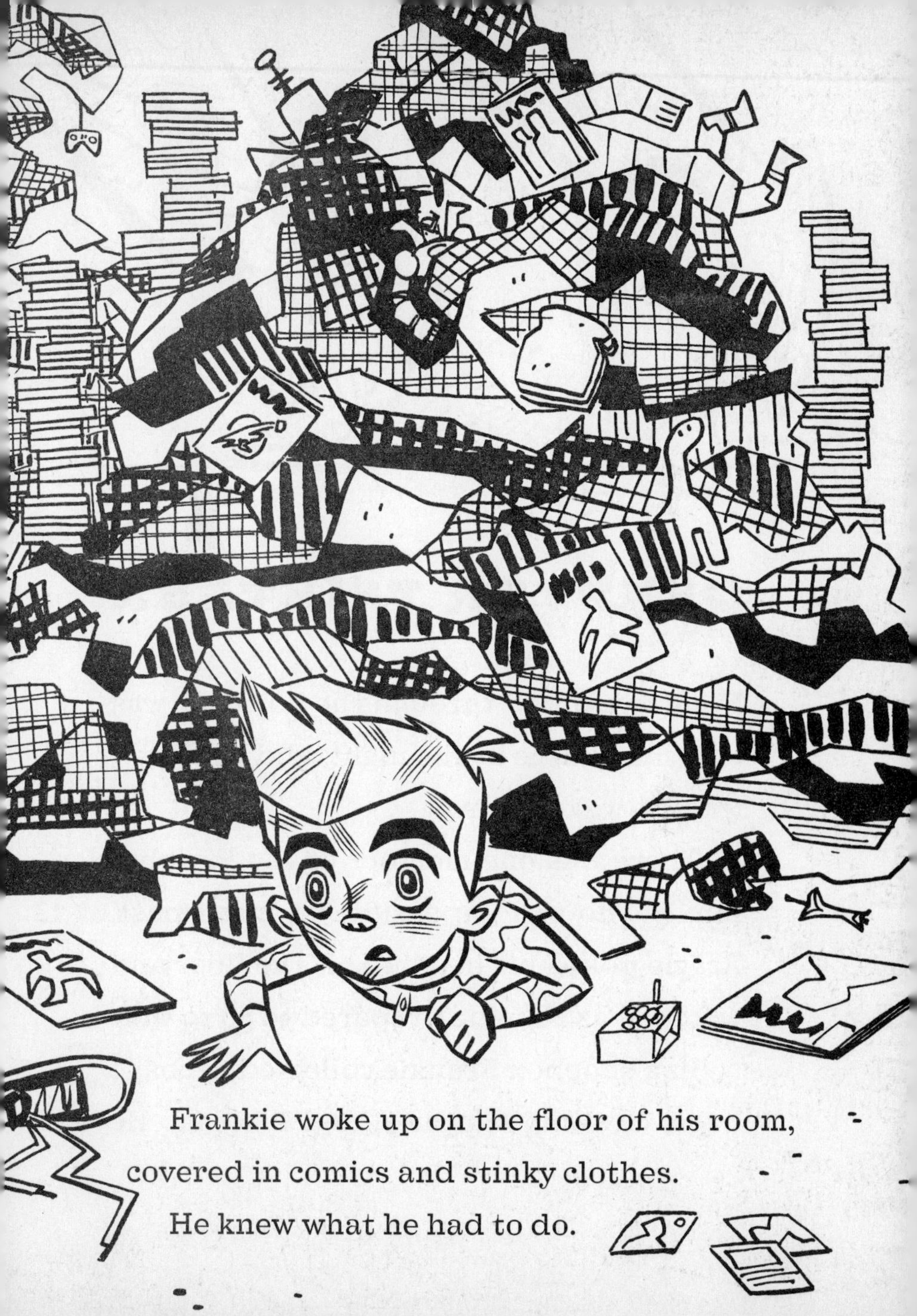

Frankie woke up on the floor of his room,
covered in comics and stinky clothes.
He knew what he had to do.

CHAPTER THIRTEEN

Frankie tiptoed through the house. It was still the middle of the night, and he didn't want to wake anyone.

There was one member of the Piccolini family who was impossible to sneak past. Argyle poked his head up off the floor and watched as Frankie prepared to go to war.

In a shoebox Frankie collected garbage bags, cleaning supplies, and a chisel. He also grabbed cookies and a juice box for nourishment.

When he got back to his room, Argyle was waiting for him with a feather duster in his teeth.

"You sure you want in?" said Frankie.

"Arf!" said Argyle.

"Okay." Frankie spritzed the air with deodorizer.

LET'S DO THIS.

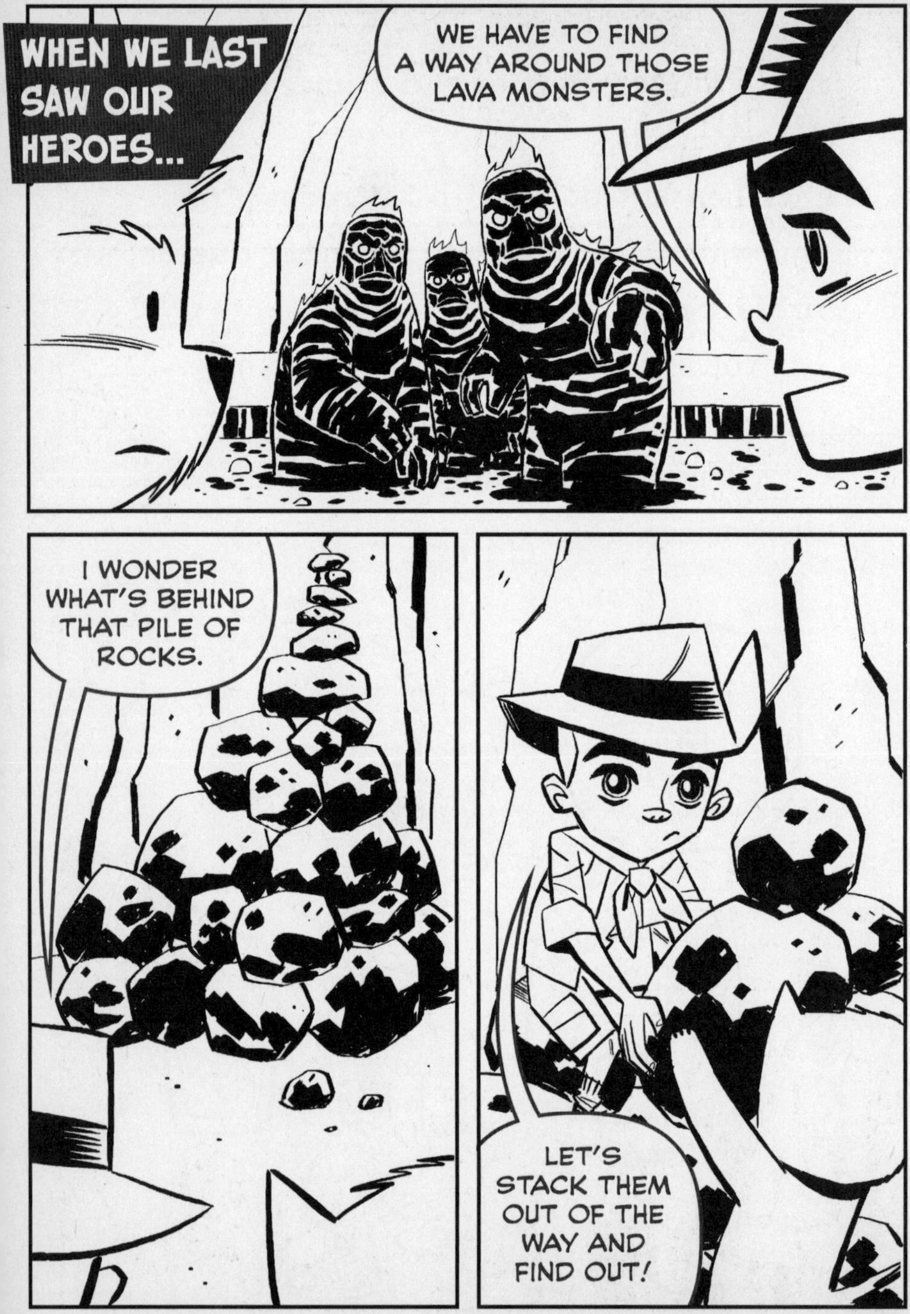

WHEN WE LAST SAW OUR HEROES...
WE HAVE TO FIND A WAY AROUND THOSE LAVA MONSTERS.
I WONDER WHAT'S BEHIND THAT PILE OF ROCKS.
LET'S STACK THEM OUT OF THE WAY AND FIND OUT!

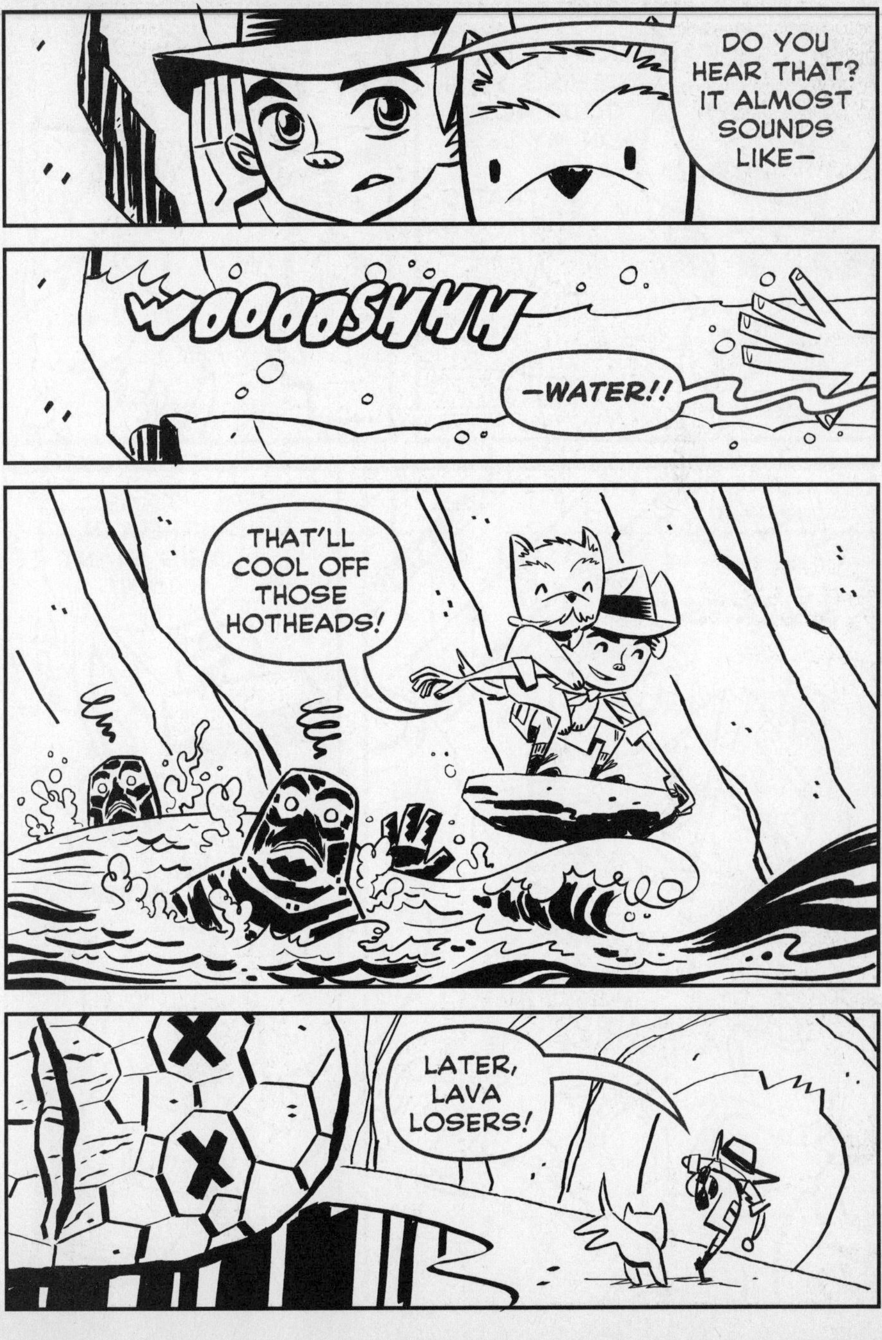
DO YOU HEAR THAT? IT ALMOST SOUNDS LIKE—
WOOOOOSHHHH
—WATER!!
THAT'LL COOL OFF THOSE HOTHEADS!
LATER, LAVA LOSERS!

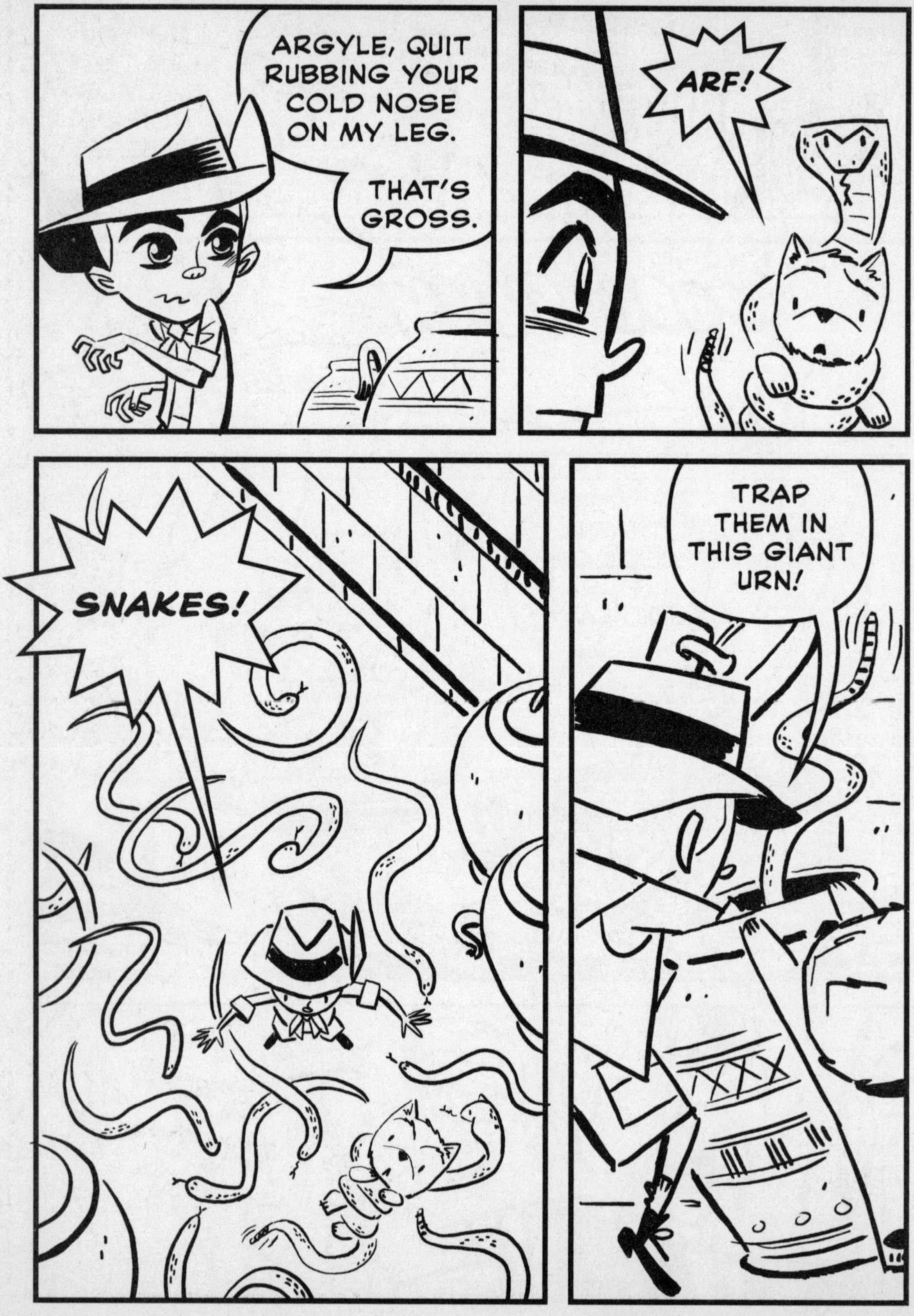
ARGYLE, QUIT RUBBING YOUR COLD NOSE ON MY LEG.
THAT'S GROSS.
ARF!
SNAKES!
TRAP THEM IN THIS GIANT URN!

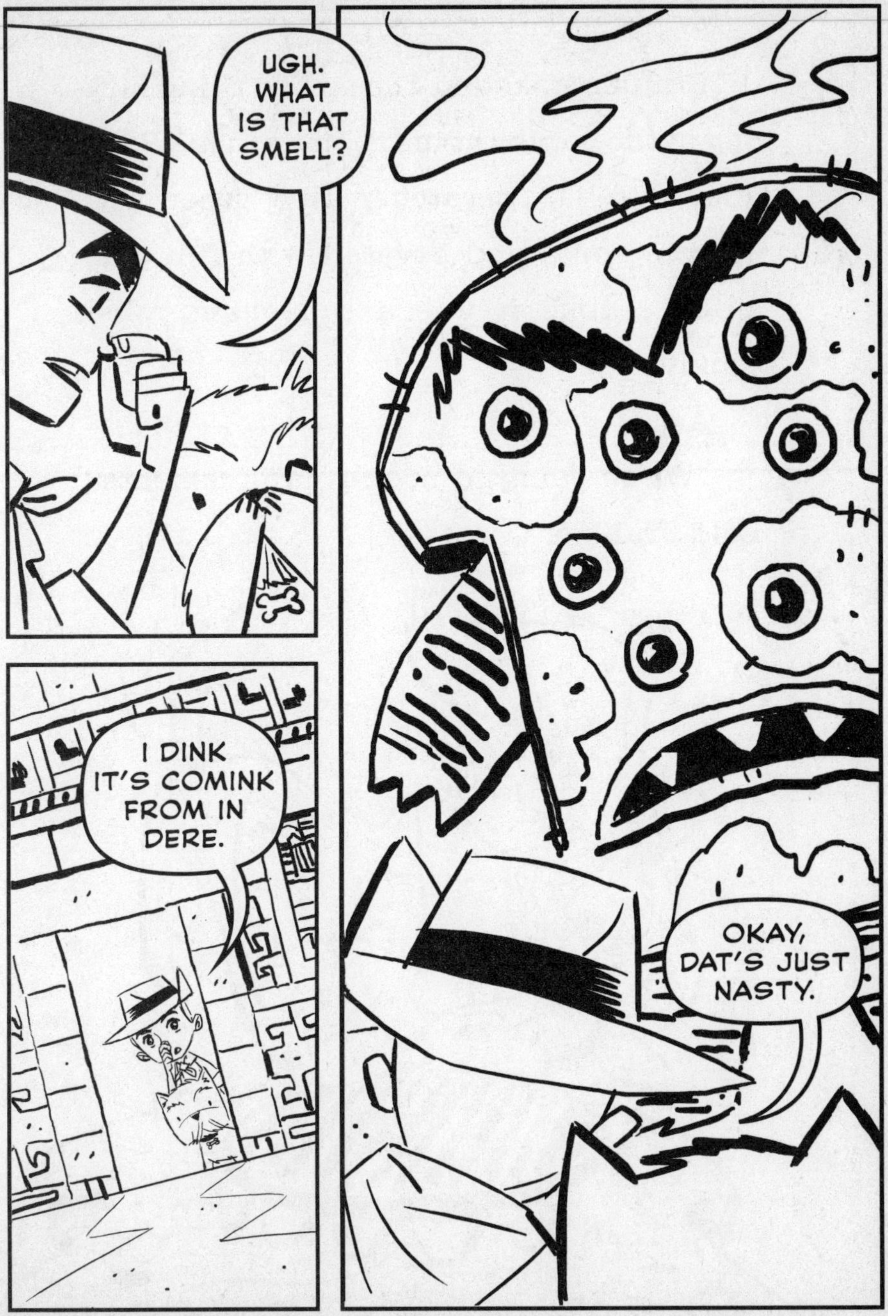
UGH. WHAT IS THAT SMELL?
I DINK IT'S COMINK FROM IN DERE.
OKAY, DAT'S JUST NASTY.

Frankie poked at the smelly thing lurking in the corner of his room with his Peter Platypus back-scratcher. Now green with purple spots and covered with fur, once upon a time it was a salami-and-relish sandwich.

Argyle gagged.

"We're going to need reinforcements," said Frankie.

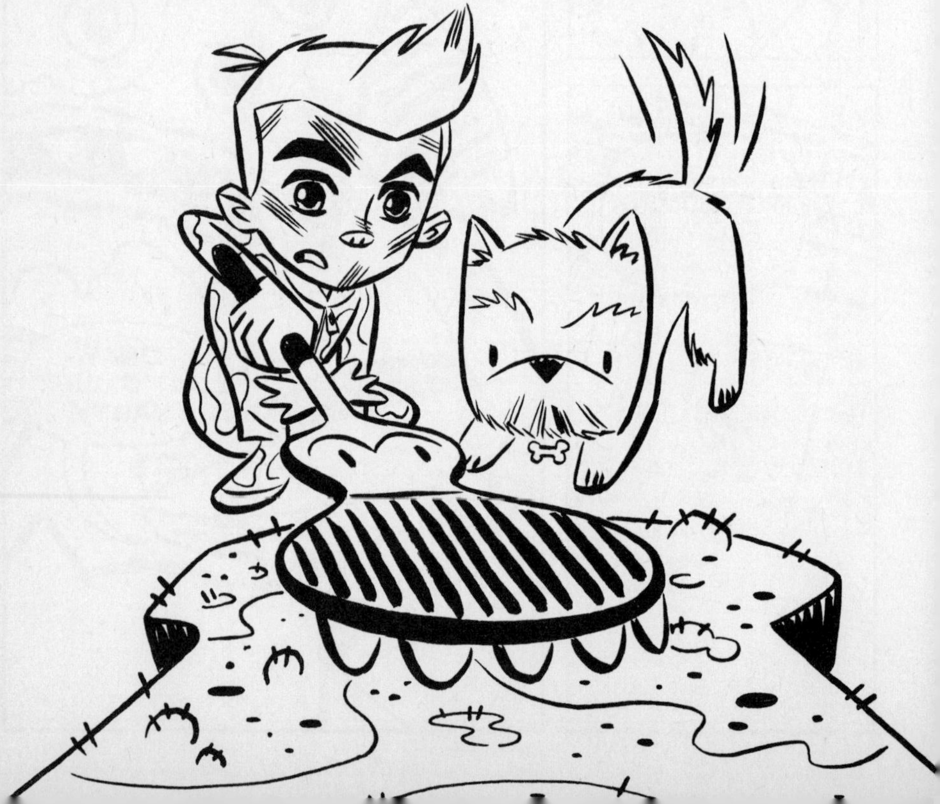

CHAPTER FOURTEEN

Frankie hurried out of his room, return-
ing a minute later wearing a hockey mask
and yellow dish gloves. He gripped a plastic zipper-top bag in one hand and a beach
shovel in the other.

"Cover me. I'm going in," he said.

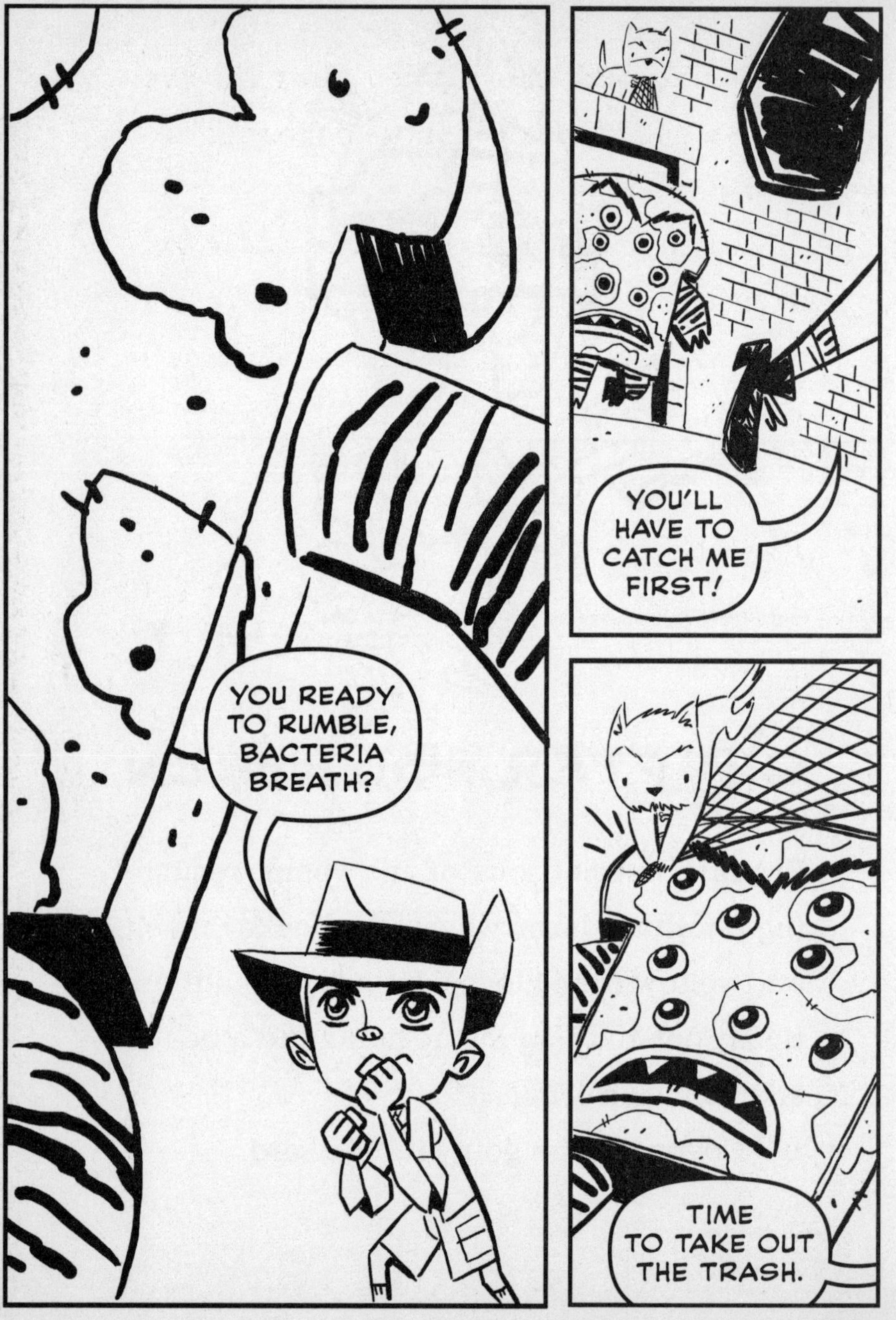
YOU READY TO RUMBLE, BACTERIA BREATH?
YOU'LL HAVE TO CATCH ME FIRST!
TIME TO TAKE OUT THE TRASH.

Frankie slid the zipper shut on the plastic bag. “Locks in not-so-freshness,” he said.

Now that the mold monster had been defeated, there was only one challenge left to tackle: the Closet. He turned the knob ever so slowly, trying not to think about the danger that awaited them on the other side.

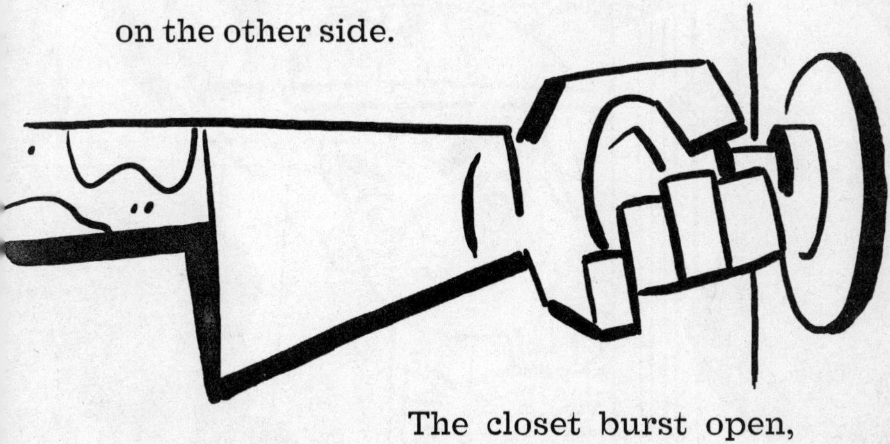

The closet burst open, erupting like a volcano. Comics, toys, games, and more spilled out all over the floor. Argyle yelped as he jumped out of the way.

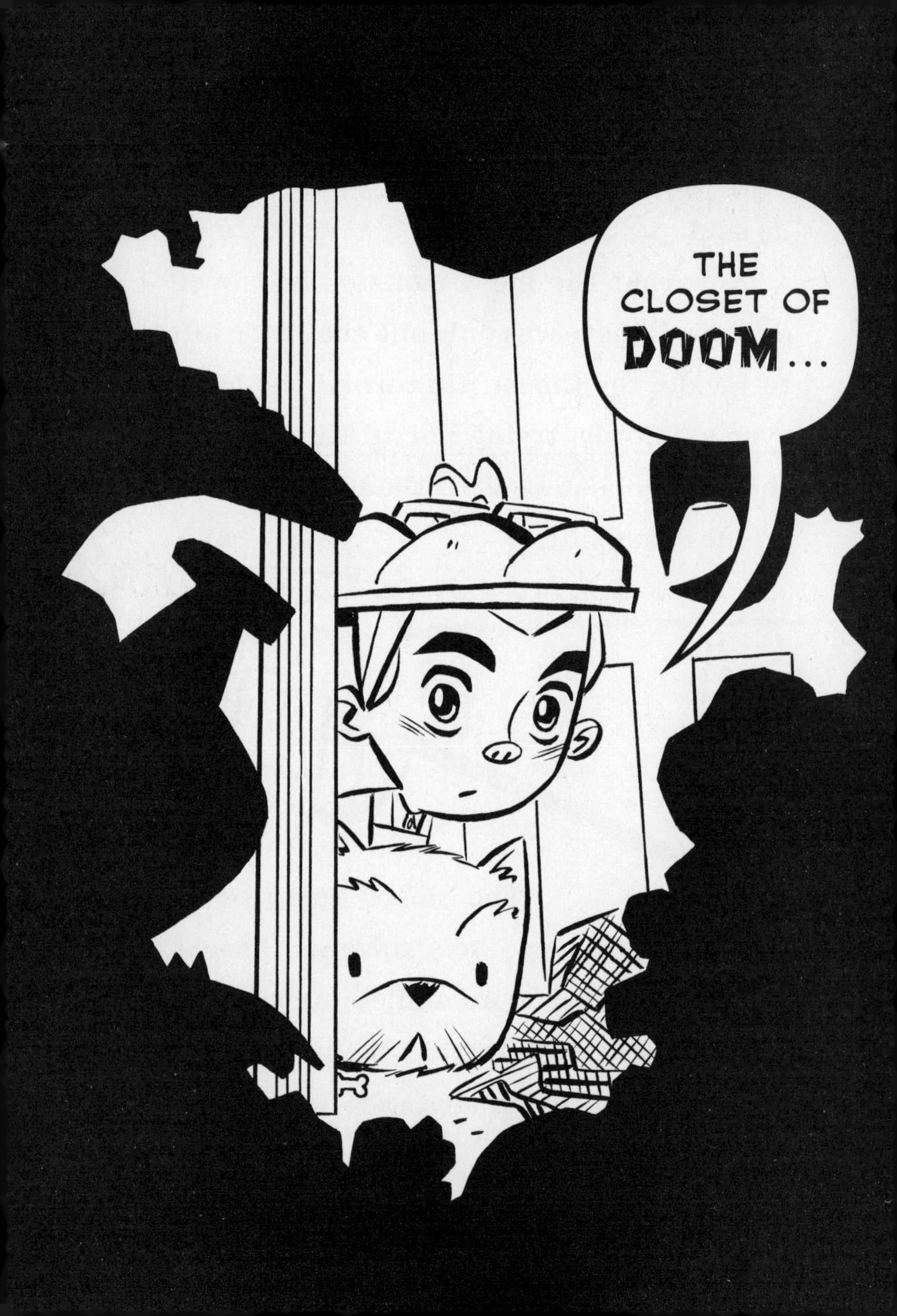
THE CLOSET OF DOOM...

CHAPTER FIFTEEN

Most Saturdays, the Piccolini family woke to the sweet aroma of Dad's doughy delights. Not today. This time, the whir of a vacuum cleaner got them out of bed.

Everyone sleepily followed the noise to Frankie's room. What they saw woke them up like a bucket of cold water.

Frankie's room was a museum of awesome.

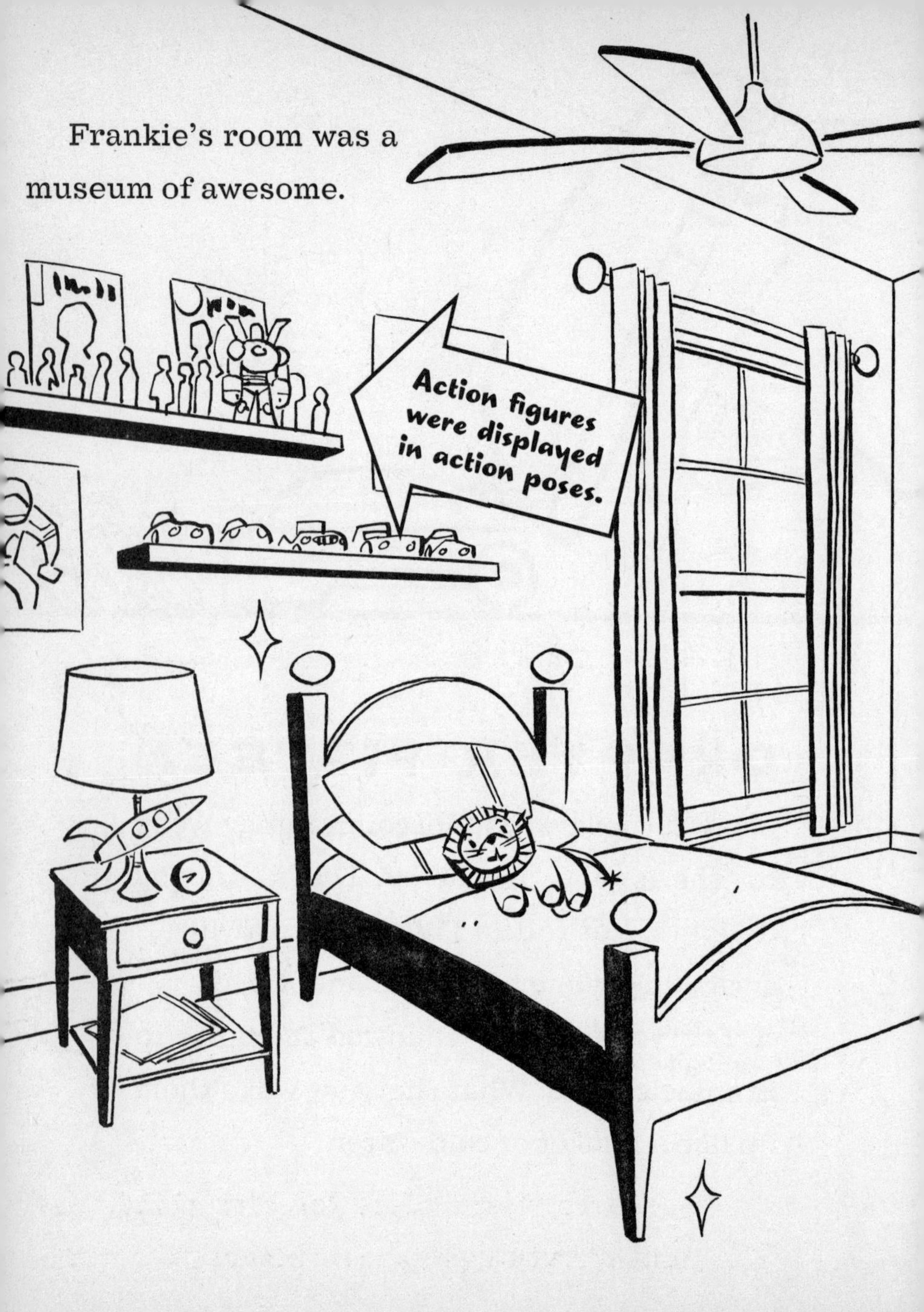
Action figures were displayed in action poses.

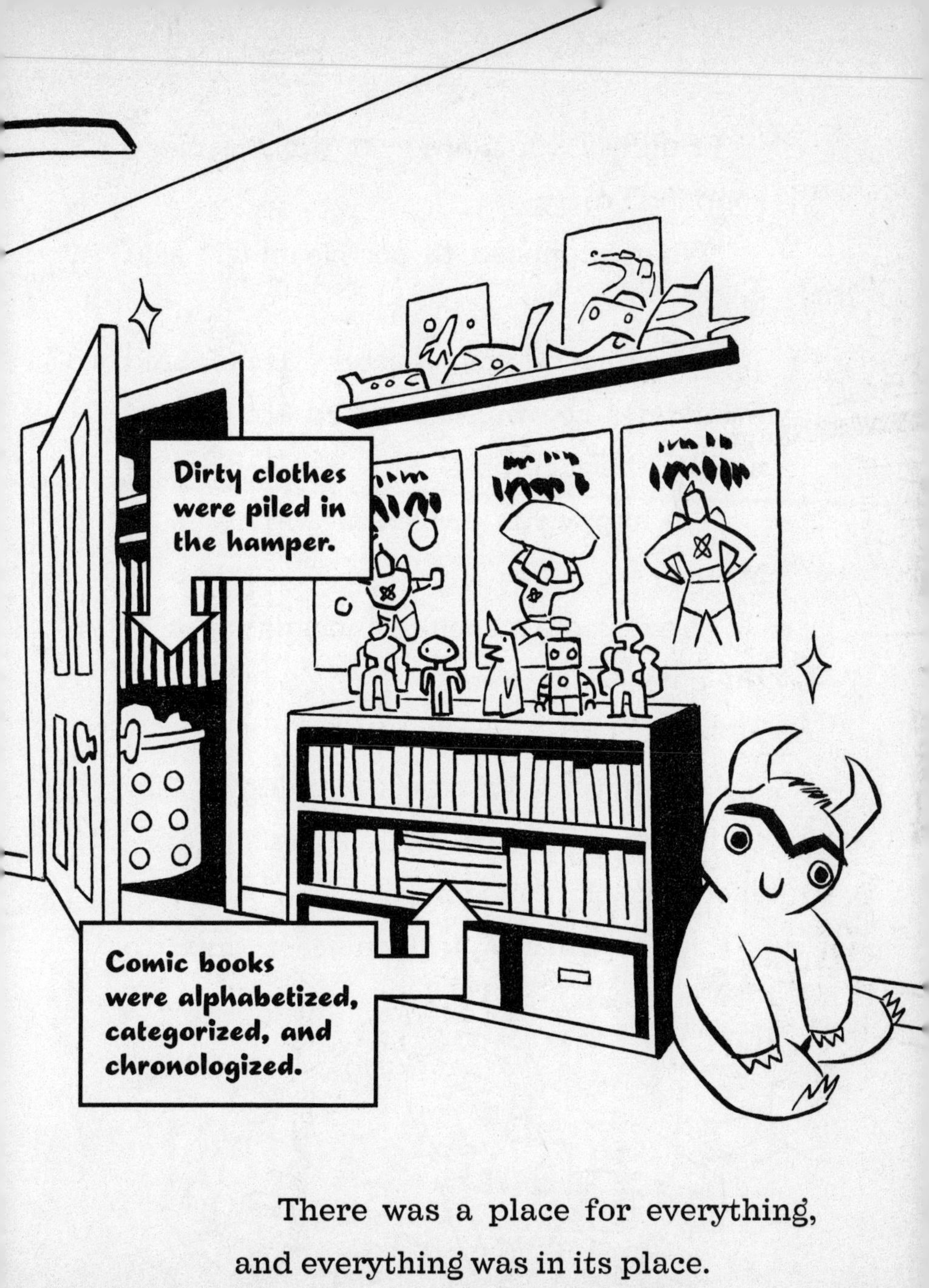
Dirty clothes were piled in the hamper.
Comic books were alphabetized, categorized, and chronologized.

There was a place for everything,
and everything was in its place.

Frankie's room was so tidy, it made soap look dirty.

"What happened to not cleaning?" said Mom.

"Not one of your better ideas," said Frankie as he wound the cord around the neck of the vacuum.

"I'm happy you proved me wrong," said Mom.

"Wow, Bro. You really knocked it out of the park," said Piper.

"Coo," Lucy agreed.

Dad patted Frankie's shoulder. "How about we celebrate with some banana-chocolate chip pancakes?"

"There's still one last thing to clean," said Frankie.

CHAPTER SIXTEEN

Frankie took the longest, hottest, steami-
est bubble bath of his entire life. It felt
good. He had been so dirty that the water
turned brown, like milk did from Frosted
Cocoa Loops.

Later at breakfast, the phone rang.

Frankie got to it first. On the other end of the line was the sound of an oboe.

"Hi, Kenny," said Frankie. "Yeah, I can't wait for you to see it."

Frankie hung up the phone and rejoined everyone at the breakfast table.

"You must be excited to show off your room to Kenny," said Dad.

"And get it all messed up?" said Frankie. "No way. I'm going to play over at his house."

"Then what were you so anxious about?" said Mom.

Frankie pulled a zipper-top bag out of his pocket. In it was something square, purplish green, and furry: the thing that used to be a salami-and-relish sandwich.

"Kenny and I are going to check this out under his microscope," said Frankie.

"Ewwww!" said everyone at the same time.

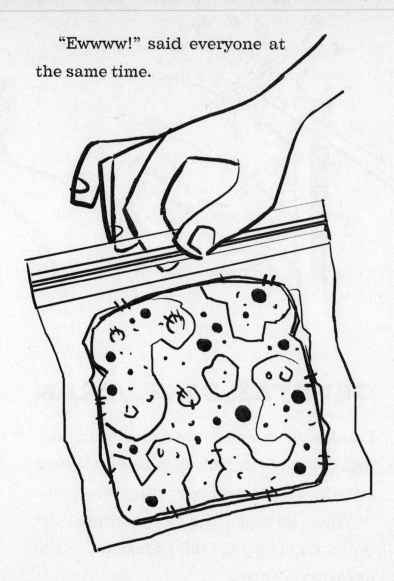

CHAPTER SEVENTEEN

Frankie slept well in his clean room that night. So well, in fact, that he didn't even stir when the Dryer Sheet Fairy returned.

When he woke the next morning, he found a note by his pillow instead of the usual dryer sheet.

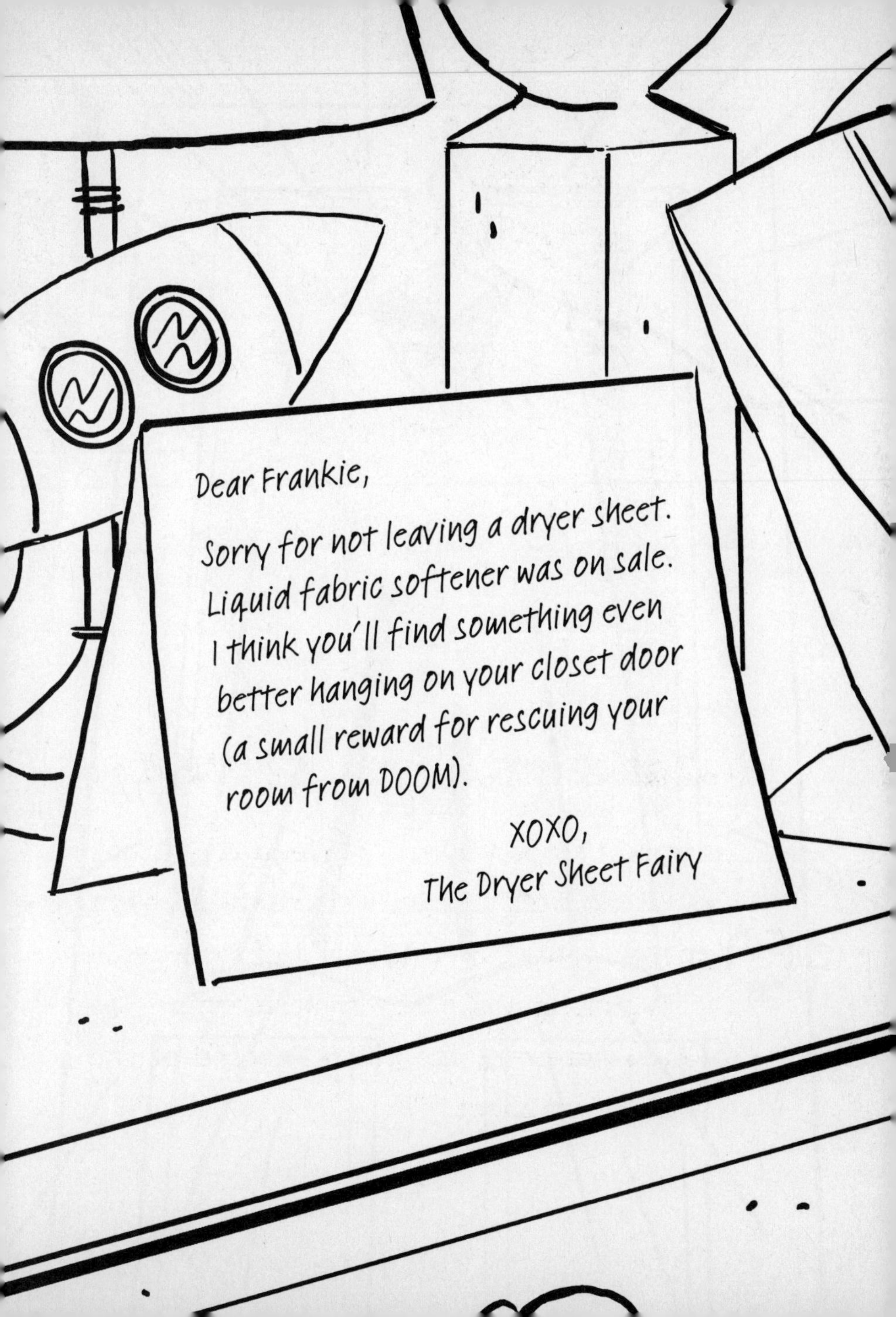
Dear Frankie,
Sorry for not leaving a dryer sheet.
Liquid fabric softener was on sale.
I think you'll find something even
better hanging on your closet door
(a small reward for rescuing your
room from DOOM).
XOXO,
The Dryer Sheet Fairy

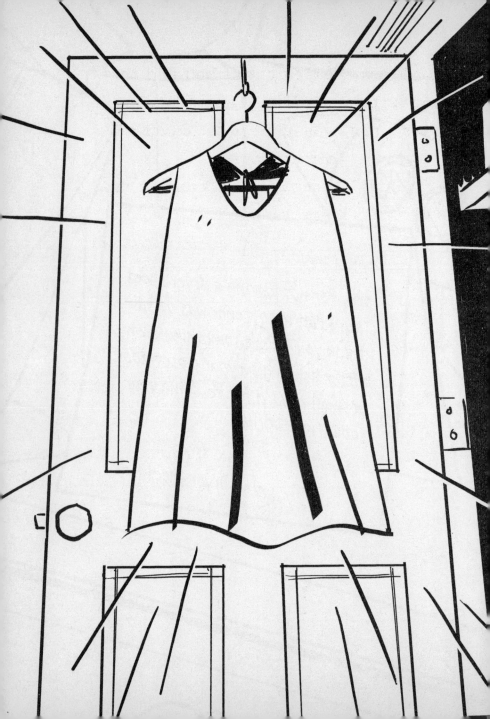

Frankie leaped out of bed and threw open the closet. Hanging on a hook inside was a rectangle of green satin fabric. His very own superhero cape!

He tied it around his neck and admired himself in the mirror.

Then Frankie dashed out of his room in search of his next adventure.

HOW TO DRAW FRANKIE

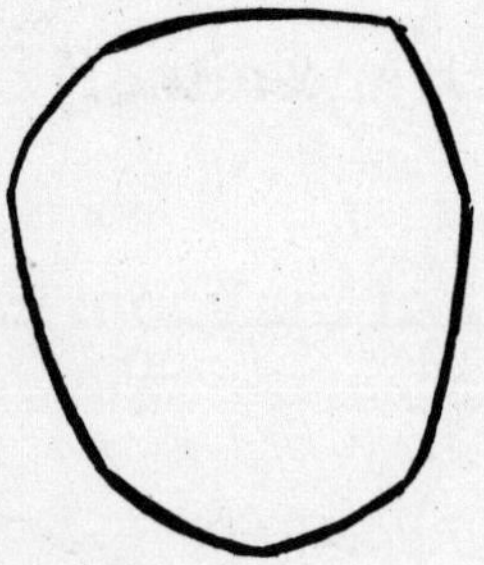

1.

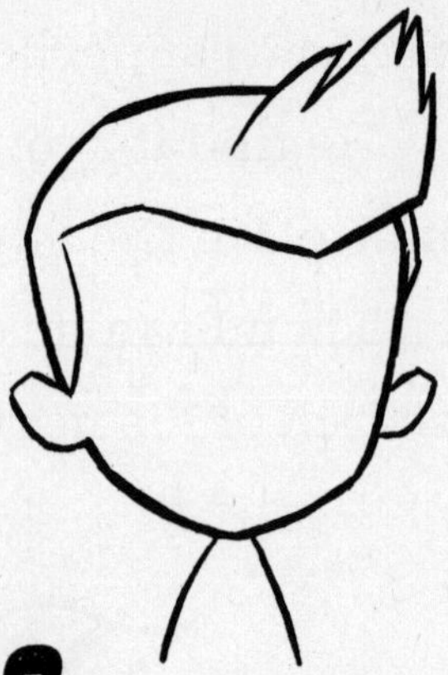

2.

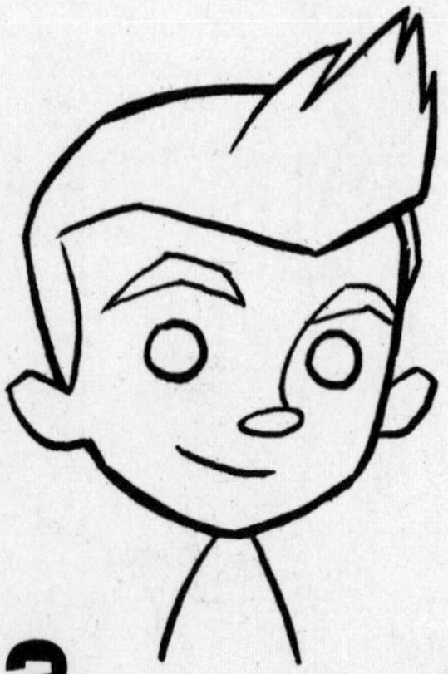

3.

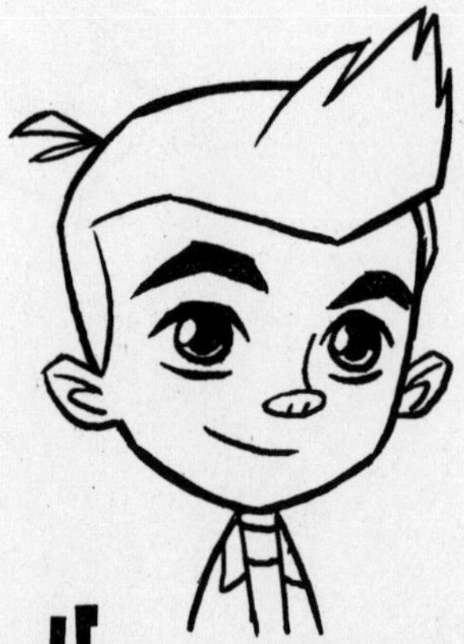

4.

HOW TO DRAW ARGYLE

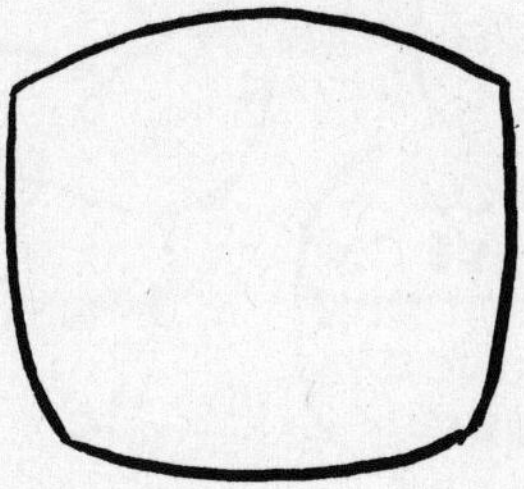

1.

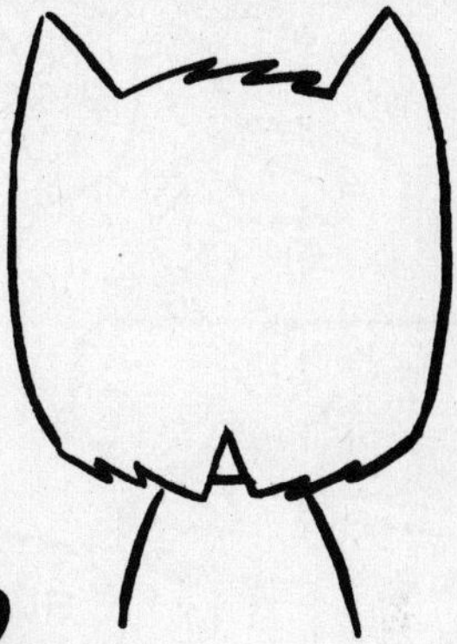

2.

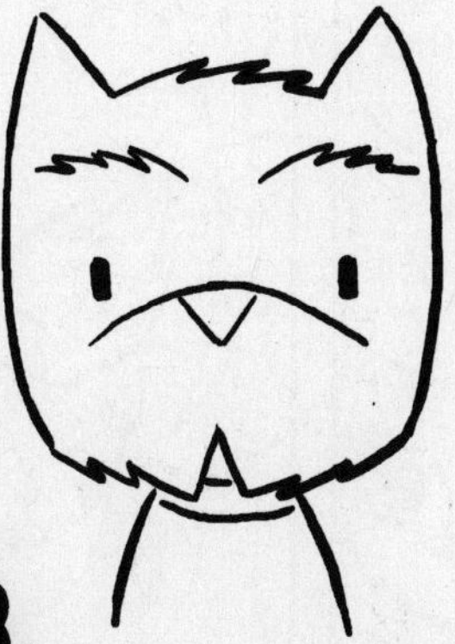

3.

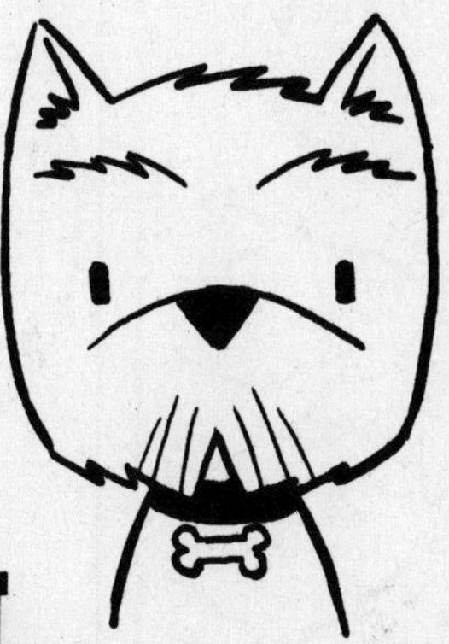

4.

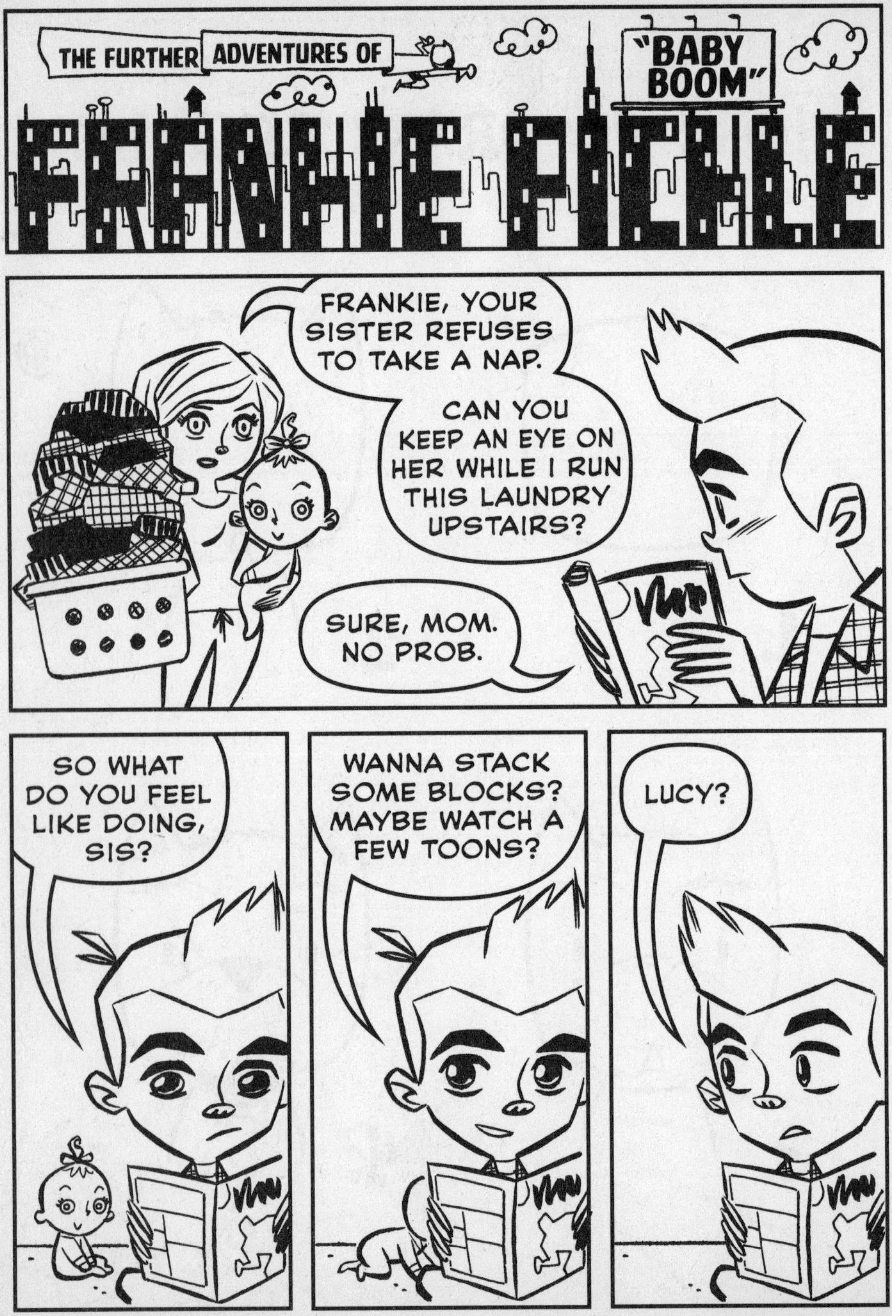
THE FURTHER ADVENTURES OF
FRANKIE PICKLE
"BABY BOOM"
FRANKIE, YOUR SISTER REFUSES TO TAKE A NAP.
CAN YOU KEEP AN EYE ON HER WHILE I RUN THIS LAUNDRY UPSTAIRS?
SURE, MOM. NO PROB.
SO WHAT DO YOU FEEL LIKE DOING, SIS?
WANNA STACK SOME BLOCKS? MAYBE WATCH A FEW TOONS?
LUCY?

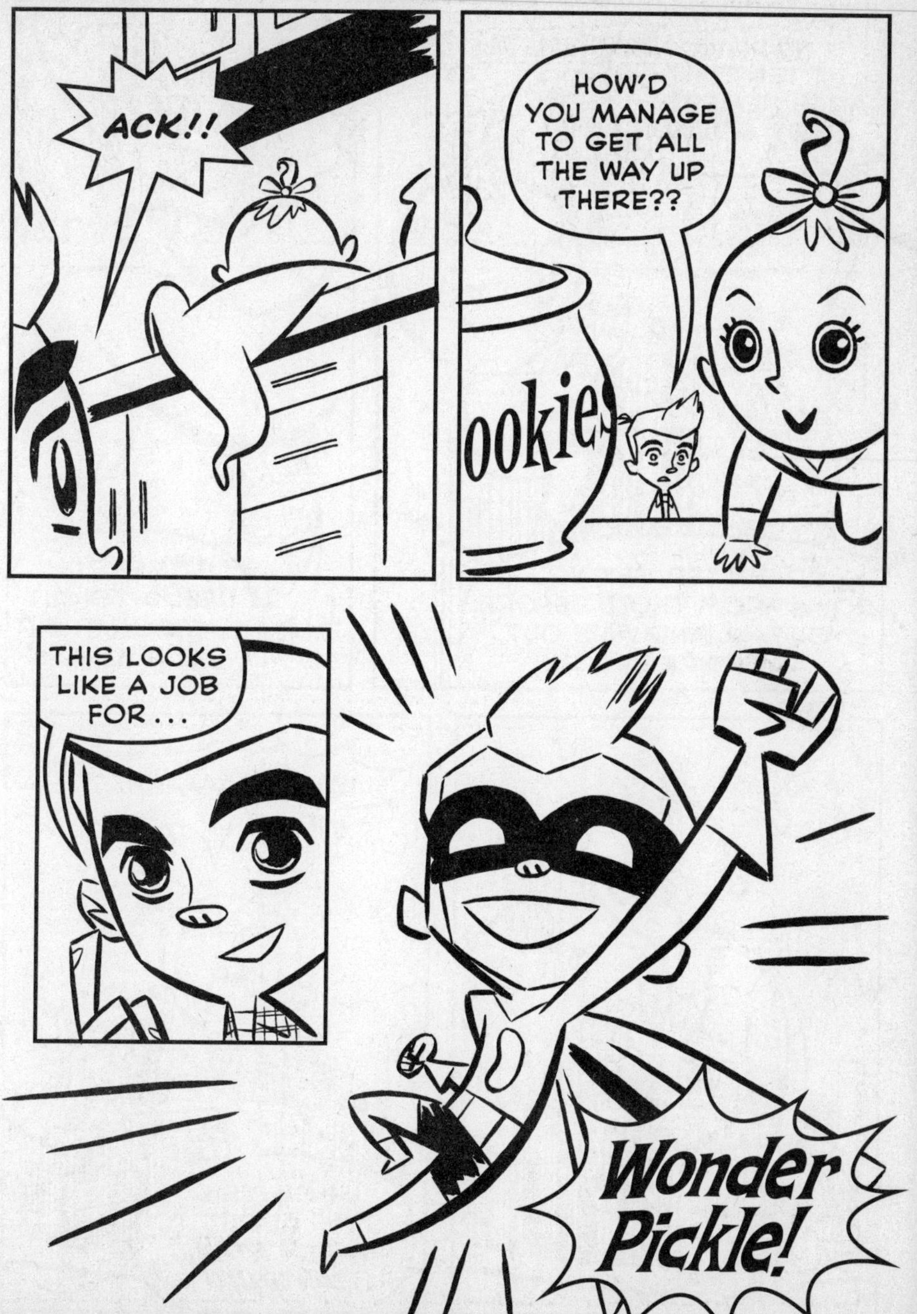
ACK!!
HOW'D YOU MANAGE TO GET ALL THE WAY UP THERE??
ookies
THIS LOOKS LIKE A JOB FOR . . .
Wonder Pickle!

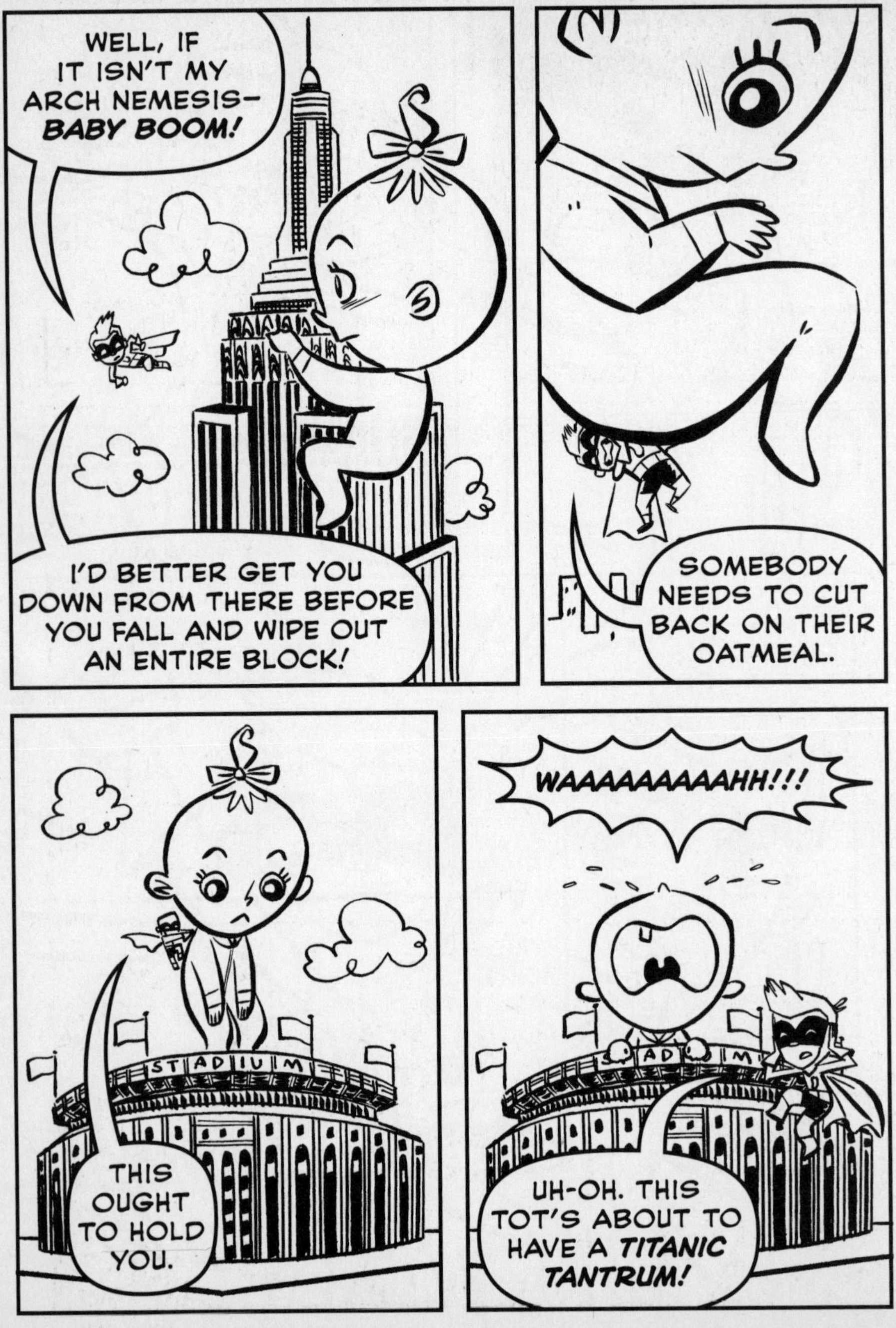
WELL, IF IT ISN'T MY ARCH NEMESIS- *BABY BOOM!*
I'D BETTER GET YOU DOWN FROM THERE BEFORE YOU FALL AND WIPE OUT AN ENTIRE BLOCK!
SOMEBODY NEEDS TO CUT BACK ON THEIR OATMEAL.
STADIUM
THIS OUGHT TO HOLD YOU.
WAAAAAAAAAHH!!!
UH-OH. THIS TOT'S ABOUT TO HAVE A *TITANIC TANTRUM!*

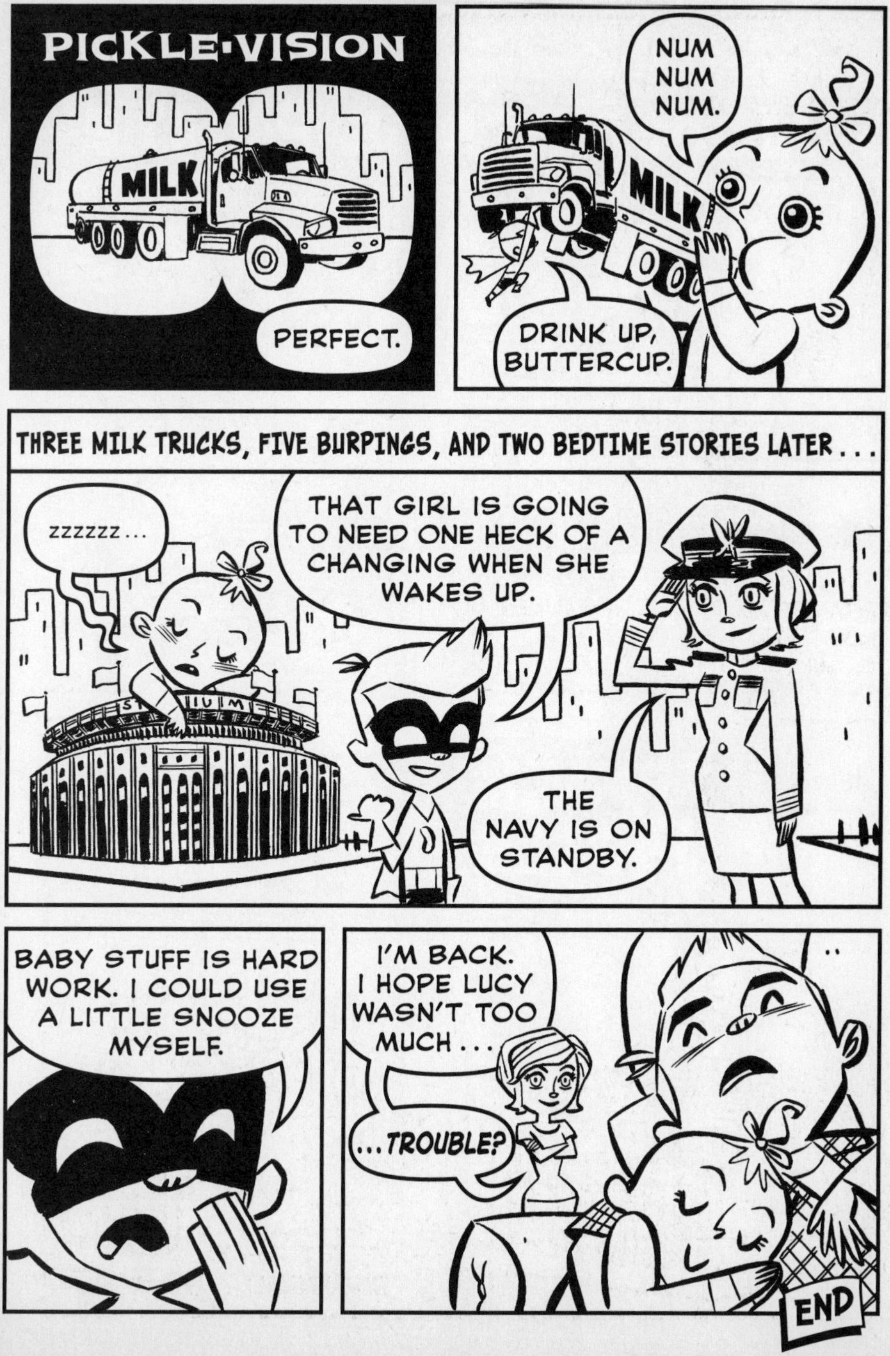
PICKLE·VISION
MILK
PERFECT.
NUM NUM NUM.
MILK
DRINK UP, BUTTERCUP.
THREE MILK TRUCKS, FIVE BURPINGS, AND TWO BEDTIME STORIES LATER . . .
ZZZZZZ . . .
THAT GIRL IS GOING TO NEED ONE HECK OF A CHANGING WHEN SHE WAKES UP.
THE NAVY IS ON STANDBY.
BABY STUFF IS HARD WORK. I COULD USE A LITTLE SNOOZE MYSELF.
I'M BACK. I HOPE LUCY WASN'T TOO MUCH . . .
. . . TROUBLE?
END

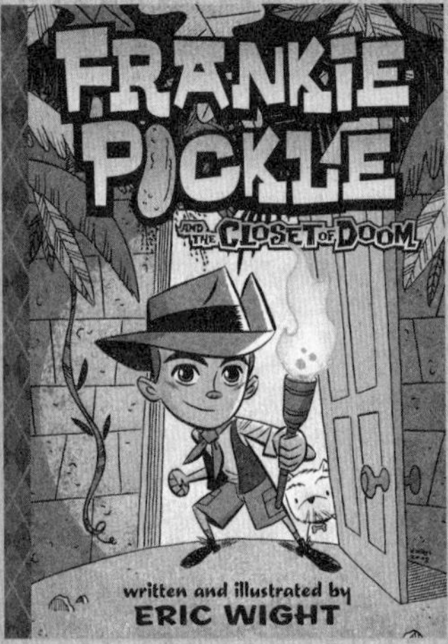
FRANKIE PICKLE
AND THE CLOSET OF DOOM
written and illustrated by
ERIC WIGHT

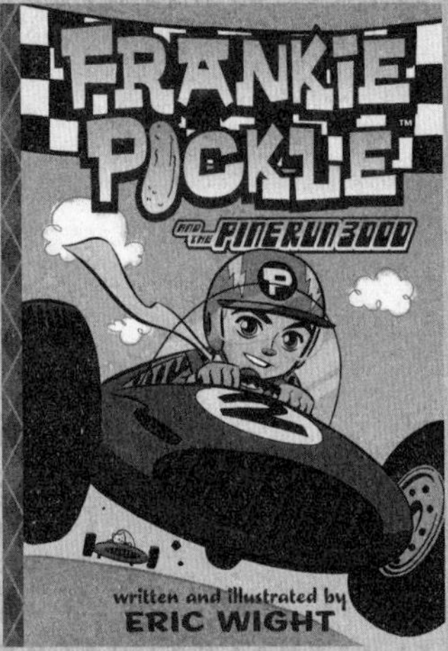
FRANKIE PICKLE™
AND THE PINE RUN 3000
written and illustrated by
ERIC WIGHT

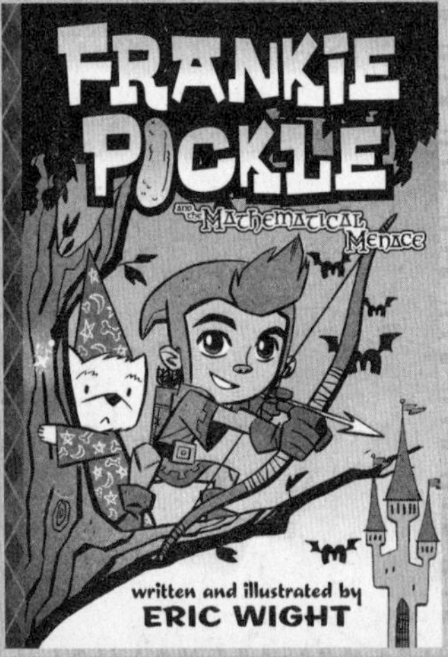
FRANKIE PICKLE
AND THE MATHEMATICAL MENACE
written and illustrated by
ERIC WIGHT

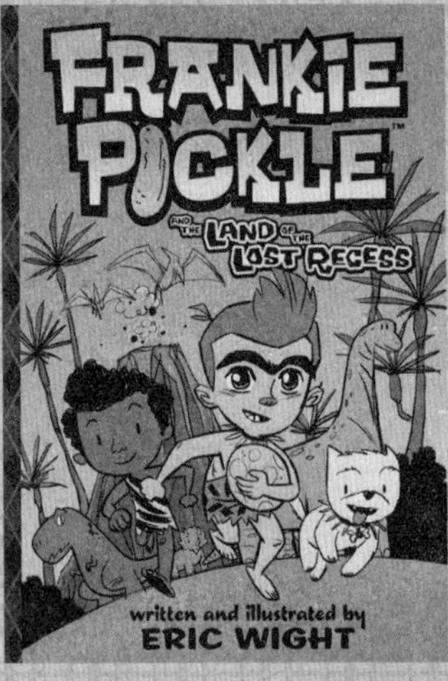
FRANKIE PICKLE™
AND THE LAND OF THE LOST RECESS
written and illustrated by
ERIC WIGHT

JIM BENTON
FRANNY K. STEIN
MAD SCIENTIST

WHO SAID SCIENCE WAS BORING?

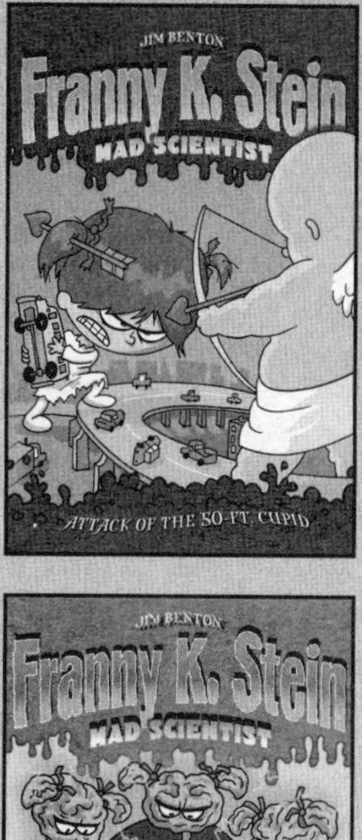
JIM BENTON
Franny K. Stein
MAD SCIENTIST
ATTACK OF THE 50-FT. CUPID

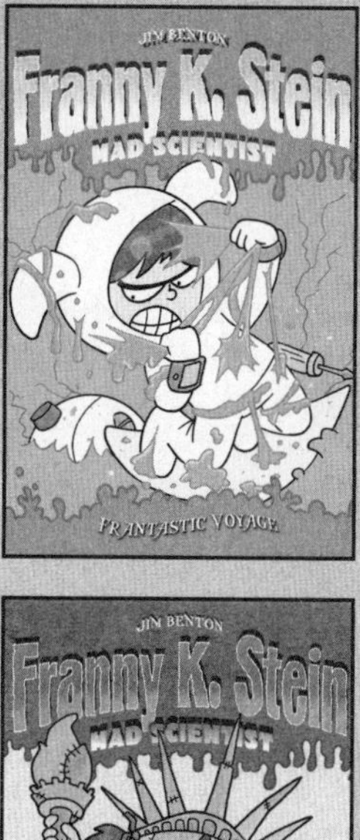
JIM BENTON
Franny K. Stein
MAD SCIENTIST
FRANTASTIC VOYAGE

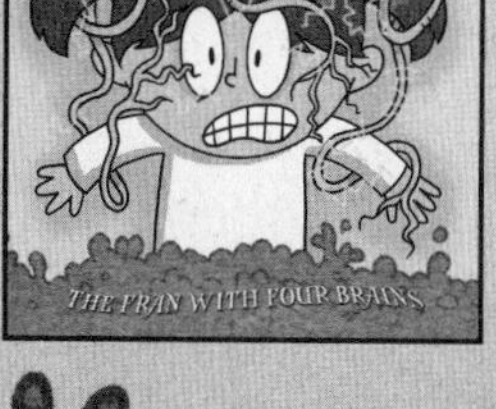
JIM BENTON
Franny K. Stein
MAD SCIENTIST
THE FRAN WITH FOUR BRAINS

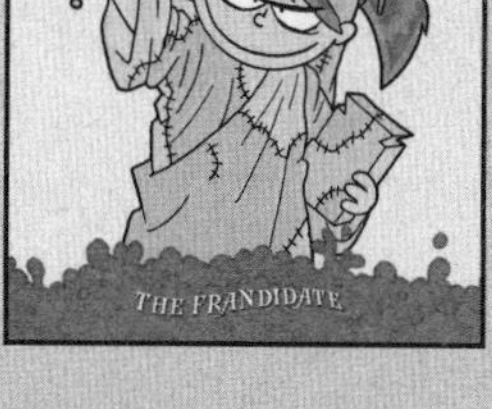
JIM BENTON
Franny K. Stein
MAD SCIENTIST
THE FRANDIDATE

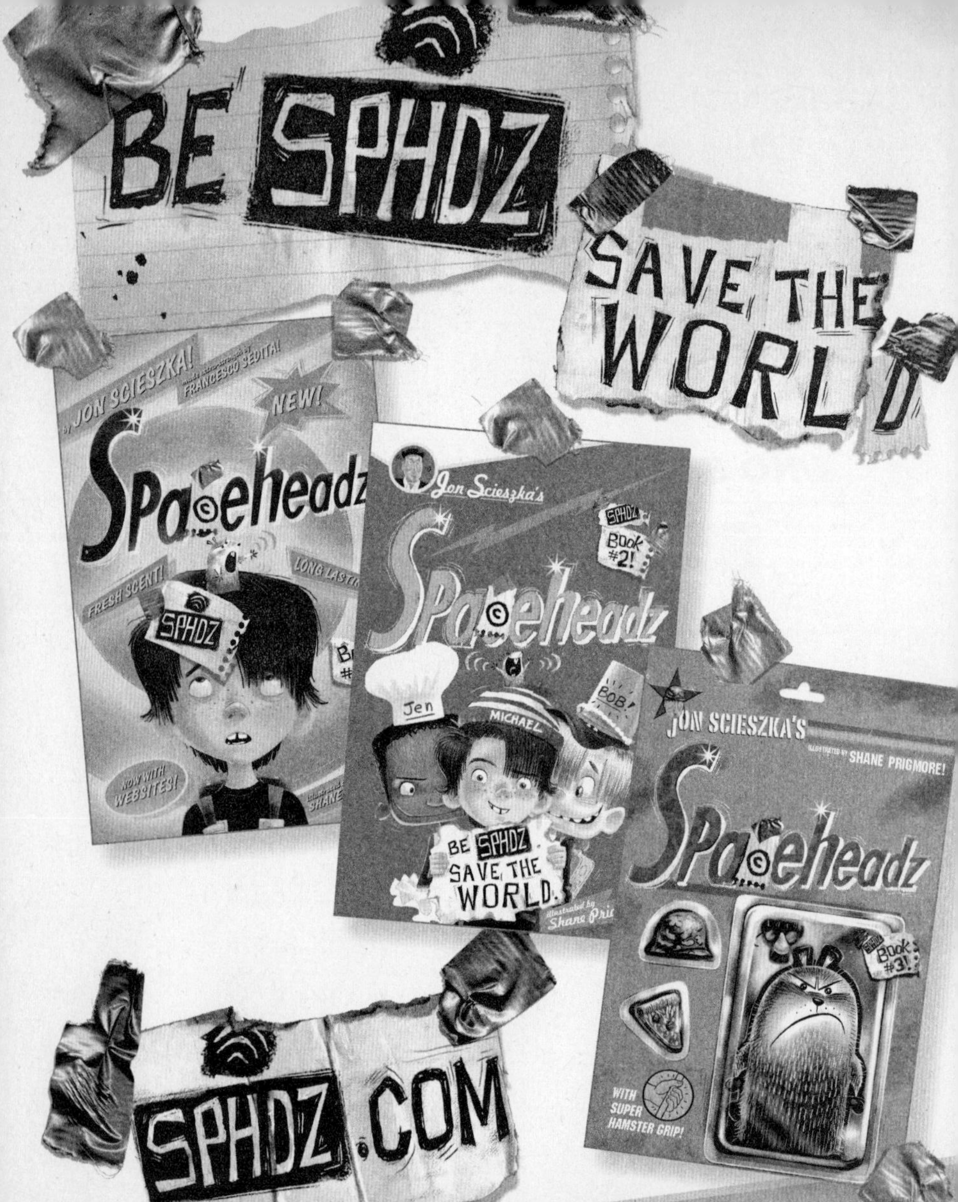
BE SPHDZ
SAVE THE WORLD
JON SCIESZKA!
FRANCESCO SEDITA!
NEW!
Spaceheadz
FRESH SCENT!
SPHDZ
NOW WITH WEBSITES!
Jon Scieszka's
Spaceheadz
SPHDZ BOOK #2!
Jen
MICHAEL
BOB!
BE SPHDZ SAVE THE WORLD.
JON SCIESZKA'S
SHANE PRIGMORE!
Spaceheadz
BOOK #3!
WITH SUPER HAMSTER GRIP!
SPHDZ.COM